Into the
Wasteland

Into the Wasteland

Lesley Choyce

Red Deer Press

Published in Canada by Red Deer Press, 195 Allstate Parkway, Markham, Ontario L3R 4T8
Published in the United States by Red Deer Press, 311 Washington Street, Brighton, Massachusetts 02135

www.reddeerpress.com

10 9 8 7 6 5 4 3 2 1

Red Deer Press acknowledges with thanks the Canada Council for the Arts, and the Ontario Arts Council for their support of our publishing program. We acknowledge the financial support of the Government of Canada through the Canada Book Fund (CBF) for our publishing activities.

 **Canada Council Conseil des Arts
for the Arts du Canada**

 ONTARIO ARTS COUNCIL
CONSEIL DES ARTS DE L'ONTARIO
an Ontario government agency
un organisme du gouvernement de l'Ontario

Library and Archives Canada Cataloguing in Publication
Choyce, Lesley, 1951-, author
    Into the wasteland / Lesley Choyce.
Issued in print and electronic formats.
ISBN 978-0-88995-522-6 (pbk.).--ISBN 978 1 55244-336-1 (epub).--
ISBN 978-1-55244-337-8 (pdf)
    I. Title.
PS8555.H668I68 2014   jC813'.54   C2014-904736-3
                                              C2014-904737-1
Publisher Cataloging-in-Publication Data (U.S.)
Choyce, Lesley.
    Into the wasteland / Lesley Choyce.
[216] pages : cm.
Summary: Dixon Carter begins a diary the day he decides to give up his meds; he's bipolar, thus suffers from the characteristic highs and lows. He starts out angry at the world, convinced he's the brightest one around, but when his best friend unexpectedly dies, he has to shift gears and try to sort out not only the meaning of the death, but also the meaning of his own life and what he should be doing with it.
ISBN-13: 978-0-88995-522-6 (pbk.)
Also published in electronic formats.
1. Manic-depressive illness – Juvenile fiction. 2. Youth and death – Juvenile fiction. I. Title.
[Fic] dc23   PZ7.C4593In 2014

Edited for the Press by Peter Carver
Cover and text design by Daniel Choi
Cover image courtesy of iStock
Printed in Canada by Friesens Corporation

 MIX
Paper from
responsible sources
FSC® C016245

PROLOGUE

In order for you to fully understand me, Dixon Carter, I need to take you back, back to who I was at the start. Because of my condition, I had been taking medication daily so I could keep from going crazy, go to school, and act normal. But then I decided to stop taking those drugs. I began a journal for some imaginary reader and I guess that reader is you. My journal takes you up to Day 9. And then it stops. You'll see why. I couldn't go back and pick up the story for a long time after that, as you'll see. In fact, I had given up on you, my imaginary reader, altogether. And I'd given up on myself. But then things happened that changed everything and I thought of you again and realized that a story without an ending is in itself a tragedy.

I'm sorry, but I needed to take you down a dark path. I needed to rant and shout at you and tell you things that you may not want to hear. I was on a journey to the heart of the wasteland; that's all I can tell you at the outset. With that said, there's nowhere to begin but at the beginning.

DAY

ONE

I think we are in rats' alley
Where the dead men lost their bones.

I'm giving notice right now that I'm not taking any shit anymore.

Yeah, you heard me right. I'm done. Through. Finished. I'm on the edge of something and I don't know what it is. I just know that everything and everybody is holding me back. I'm not saying I'm right or that I'm smarter or any of that. I just need to be free from restraint. I need to start over. I need to start something. I need to free myself from what I've been conditioned to believe.

Yeah, right. Who the hell do I think I am, that I can just stop playing by the rules, living by the code, breaking off from tradition?

Well, that's just it. I'm nobody. Nobody in particular. I see through the illusions we live by. Maybe that, too, is an illusion. If so, it is one of my own making. So I have to make up a new set of rules or maybe no rules at all.

Who needs rules? Just idiots, robots, airheads, and screw-ups, and lazy minds by the millions.

I guess you see a little anger here. Who am I angry at, you might ask?

I'm angry at pretty much everyone.

From this moment on, I am my own person, my own nation, my own religion. My own self.

No, I do not want followers. What a pain in the ass that would be. And I don't want to change the world. Not right now, anyway. I need to figure some shit out. Yeah, really figure some things out. And I don't expect it will be pretty.

This is not going to be tidy or succinct. I've been wallowing, okay? Wallowing in self-pity, self-righteousness, self-absorbed gloom, selfishness, and stubbornness. I've got a bit more of all that to do yet. So if you are along for the ride, okay, but I'm probably going to piss you off. I've come to this point, this breaking point, this point of no return and, as a result, I'm really pissed off.

Oh, you want a list of who I'm pissed off at?

1. My parents. They don't deserve it because they are nice, boring, average, responsible people and I admit that I love them, but I have to stop living by their rules. Their rules have been handed down by this soul-sucking society we live in. They are shaped by history and culture and brainwashed like everyone. They do

not understand me and I understand that. But they need to let me evolve. Yeah, evolve. Don't laugh. It's not exactly the right word because it makes me sound like a pterodactyl or some nematode worm or maybe the next superhuman. But it is about evolution, baby. Make no bones about that.

2. My best friend, Zeke. Freakin' Zeke loves skateboarding and staring at girls and women and drinking Red Bull, and he wants to become a millionaire so he can have his own private skate park with a dozen half-pipes and a kick-ass really deep bowl. But Zeke is complex and smart and he's turned me on to poetry of all things— Allen Ginsberg and Walt Whitman and T.S. Eliot. And that's why he keeps giving me books of poetry. I get some of it but not all. Zeke also reads a lot about Celtic mythology and Arthurian legends and medieval lore. Weird, eh? Of course, he's also a bit of a stoner who knows all the names of different types of weed. But I've pissed him off talking about all this shit I'm talking about here and he doesn't want to think about it. He wants to toke and watch girls and sip RB and skate. I think that is noble in its own way but it's not for me; so I said, "Zeke, you fuckin' horny stoned toad, I love you, man, but I think there's got to be more to life than skating, energy drinks, sex, and poetry that makes no sense." And he said, "Who shoved the fork up your ass? What is it you want that's so bloody important?" And I couldn't answer him. So right now we're both pissed at each other. How stupid is that?

3. Everyone at school. Yeah, I thought I'd keep it simple. Lump them all together: teachers, kids, principal. It's a machine, school is. Designed to make us sit up straight in our seats, cut us into crisp little cookies, wrap us up in cellophane, and deliver us to some supermarket to be sold at discount. Students are victims. Teachers are victims. But I am no longer a victim. I am a warrior. (Well, I know, screw me. Warrior sounds noble and I don't know if I am noble.) But I am not about to shoot my classmates or my teachers and I don't own a gun and I don't want a gun. I am opposed to violence of any sort. And now that I've said that, I realize it's the first positive thing I've said in this manifesto (and don't roll your eyes at me for using that word. Manifesto is what this is—an evolving manifesto.). A code. An ever-evolving code to live by—but it can never be fixed, never static, always in flux, always in motion. But you've heard it here first. I don't believe in violence. So no one needs to leave the building, okay?

4. Sylvia. You may know her. Straight A's. Smartest person in school. IQ around 160. Cute. No, not cute. Classically beautiful. Shrewd but not nasty. She says she's attracted to me because I appeal to her "dark side" but she never meant that I was like evil or anything. Dark as in: brooding, cynical, big chip on my shoulder guy who is smart (yes, it is undeniable) and wickedly funny—or at least I can be when I put my mind to it. Or at least I was until I took this new turn, had this revelation, if

you will. The revelation is tentatively this: I am the only sane person in a perfectly insane world. Which is why she is currently pissed at me. And that pisses me off. I don't deserve it.

Which leads me to:

5. Just about everyone else who knows me, encounters me, or crosses my path.

DAY

TWO

Winter kept us warm, covering
Earth in forgetful snow

Now that I've got that off my chest, we can proceed. This manifesto is directed at you. I don't know who you are but it is meant to be personal, real, and epiphanic. (Yeah, you'll have to put up with my vocabulary; it's the only way I can express some things.) And it is from my head and my heart. It is not intended to be linear—you know, as in a straight line. Linear thinking is what got much of the world into the mess it is in. Linear thinking is an illusion—but then, quite possibly, everything is an illusion.

That means you and me. We are illusions, too. And it is helpful to consider this. Illusion or not, it is the hand we've been dealt till death do us part. And the good news would be that death is an illusion.

We all live forever. That's my theory. And all of what I have to say is a theory, perhaps. But it is what I believe. And what I believe is real.

If you can't handle paradox, then give up on this now. Jump off this moving bus. Blow it off. Burn it, smoke it, use it for a doorstop, or wipe your ass with it. 'Cause I've got a lot on my mind at this juncture in my life. And most of it is not easy to express.

But it will blow your mind if you can stay with it. Please.

Let me pause for a moment and take a deep breath.

Breathing is good. You get to share the atoms of oxygen with all other living things. You get to breathe molecules of nitrogen that were once in the lungs of ancient mystics and healers, of long-dead warriors and evil-doers and kind men and gentle women. And dinosaurs. You breathe the atoms that were once in the lungs of triceratops and T-Rex. So there is another mega-positive thought for your fevered forebrain. There will be more if I can discover them. So stay tuned.

A little back story might be in order.

Last year, I was a bit of a stoner. Nothing major, but I liked a little buzz. Zeke was growing some weed he called Chowder House Special in his closet at home. He was my supplier and I'd buy him some Red Bull now and then or some new trucks for his wheels. We would hang out down by the skate park or walk down to the beach and look at the waves. That's where I met Fairweather Dave.

Yes, you know who I mean. Dave Fairweather was his name, although he preferred reversing the names for some reason no one understood. Now he went by Fairweather or Fair or FWD. The name didn't really have anything to do with the weather.

Once upon a time, Dave Fairweather had been a surfing champion. A true surf champ, a pro; he shaped surfboards and then got greedy and promoted surf clothes and then skateboards and skate gear, and ended up losing interest in actually surfing and instead started making dump-truckloads of money. He rode the wave of capitalism instead of the waves at the beach. He had his own worldwide company selling mostly clothes and crap.

Then something happened. And he quit it all. He gave away a lot of his money and let other people run his company for him. He started living in his camper van along the shoreline wherever he could stay without getting hassled. Zeke would lay some free weed on him and he'd wax eloquent as he waxed his board. (Groan, yeah, go ahead—but it's my story, dude.)

"I like it when people call me just Fair," he said as he exhaled some Chowder House Special smoke. "Fair is an important word. Fair is what life should be, what people should be, what the world should be."

"That is so true," Zeke said, spinning the wheels of his skateboard with his index finger.

"But so much of life is not fair. All that money I made was not fair. Other poor buggers were working their asses off, pouring asphalt or cleaning up dog shit in the park or getting all bloody in hospital emergency rooms saving lives. All I did was ride a few waves, meet some people, and say I used their product; I made it to the top and found out that it all didn't mean shit."

I had only known fragments of FWD's story. Most people made it sound like he screwed up somehow and it all flushed down the toilet. Because, hey, he looked like a bum, lived like a bum and, to most people, he sounded like a bum. But that wasn't really it.

"What changed?" I asked, wanting the real deal.

"I changed. I woke up one morning in my beach house and discovered my dog had died. Yeah, old Lucy, nineteen years old, God bless her soul, had died in her sleep. It's not that I couldn't handle her death. That old dog had lived one hell of a life. I mean, what other dog had actually ridden on a board with her beloved master on some righteous head-high point break waves?

"But something about losing Lucy made me change the way I saw the world. Something big. All the glory, all the success and attention. It had so gone to my head that I was no longer me. I had become what everyone else wanted me to be. And it was so much fun, so great for my ego. But I suddenly realized it was like someone else living my life. It wasn't me. So I started to untangle myself from it."

"You can just do that?" I asked. "Untangle yourself from ... everything?"

"Yeah, you can, you can dis-engage." He said the word

real slow as he exhaled smoke. "It's called free will. Only problem is it takes an *iron* will. And you have to make sacrifices. Lots of sacrifices."

So I guess you could say that Fairweather Dave became a kind of mentor for me. His philosophy, as he called it, had to do with paradox and irony.

"When you're up, you're really down, and when you're down, you're up," as he would say. "Up means you have all your shit together and so you don't change or want to be unhappy or have problems. So you stay there—static, stopped, dead in the water—but also protective of your happiness and paranoid that someone will take it away.

"When you're down, you are staring up, waiting for a helping hand, trying to find a way out of your downness, your predicament. Maybe you're deep underwater and the wave is holding you down until your lungs burn from lack of oxygen. And that is a worthy place to be. You learn real shit then. You confront your demons, you talk to them, negotiate with them. You struggle, you burn mental calories, and you live life as it should be lived. Everyone needs a dark night of the soul."

Well, that's a taste of FWD. I had never really come across a person like this before. A surf guru. A drop-out, long-haired, former millionaire surf champ. I didn't know if this was all saltwater draining out of his brain or something else. But FWD was the real thing. To me, at least.

He got me thinking, thinking about me.

DAY

THREE

What are the roots that clutch, what branches grow
Out of this stony rubbish?

Well, if you've gotten this far, you are brave. You are my soul brother or sister; you are patient and kind and have an open mind. I'm still not promising anything. I'm just going to give you a magical mystery tour of my life and my thoughts. I've invited you in because it gets too lonely inside there all by myself. And I guess I want to let someone else in.

I have already thought about going the hermit route. Plan A was to drop out of school, emancipate myself from my parents (although that seemed a bit cruel and cruelty is not my style), and quietly walk out of town with a backpack of essentials and live in the woods—preferably by the sea, somewhere far from here. Get back to basics. And think. Really think pure hard thoughts that would make me the one free person on the planet.

But it didn't happen; I played it out as a solid thought experiment. I visualized me doing it. I saw it as plain as day. It was like I really lived it.

And you know what?

It wasn't that great. I started talking to the cabbages I grew. I don't know why I was growing cabbages but I was. I had this great little shack somewhere—must have been New Zealand. I had this solitary life where you didn't have to go to school and study stupid shit; you didn't have to ever shop at Walmart; and you didn't pay taxes that went to buy military weapons. I lived the life I believed in, which included the following: breathing, thinking, being self-reliant, communing with nature. And all the perfect etceteras.

But then I did a fast forward and you know what? I was a lonely, senile old man with pee-stained pants and no friends. When I died, no one knew and no one cared.

And that's just not good enough. When I die, I want someone to say, "That Dixon Carter was one pure stoked prime individual who lived life to the max and was always kind and compassionate but, at the same time, didn't give a rat's ass what anyone thought about him."

But I'm not dead yet.

And I've at least temporarily ruled out being a hermit.

And I haven't divorced my parents. And I am still in school.

So what now?

Well, that is the dilemma.

Albert Einstein said that insanity was doing the same thing over and over, expecting different results. I wish I could have talked to Einstein. I wish I could have given him a high-five. Here I am at sixteen, however, doing the same things over and over. And expecting new results. I get up, go to school, hang out with Zeke, get into passionate arguments with Sylvia, and I keep waiting for revelations, for different results. That is the insane part. My expectations. But, as duly noted, I believe I am a sane person, the only truly sane person in an insane world.

So something's gotta give. I'm waiting for it. I'm waiting for the skies to open. I'm waiting for the voice of God (if there is a God). I'm waiting for the matrix to reveal itself for the flimsy stage show it really is. I'm waiting for … something.

When Einstein was sixteen, he was in Zurich and failed the exam that would allow him to get into the school he wanted, the Swiss Federal Polytechnic School. But he knew he had smarts and wasn't too discouraged. Later, he was wise enough to renounce his German citizenship so he couldn't be drafted and shoved into the hideous war Germany would unleash on Europe.

Einstein also said, "Only two things are infinite, the universe and human stupidity, and I'm not sure about the former."

Well, human stupidity brings out my dark side. Which brings me back to Sylvia. She's smarter than me but maybe a bit more conventional in her thinking. So we get into arguments. I'm the one who usually starts them. Yesterday it started out with me stating, "I don't believe there is such a thing as good or evil. Using those labels gives us an easy excuse. If you say you are fighting for a good cause, it allows you to do terrible things. So why don't we admit that we are all a mix of good and bad and there is no such thing as a person who is truly evil."

Why I wanted to get into this with someone I really care about makes no sense whatever, though maybe it's because simplistic-minded people who see the world in black and white really piss me off. But then Sylvia, of course, is anything but simplistic.

Still, my self-righteous opinions needed to be expressed. She was the one I would express them to and that often made her mad. So we would argue.

"You don't think Hitler was pure evil?" she shot back.

"No, I don't," I foolishly said. Now I was defending Hitler. "I saw his paintings. He painted pictures of flowers. He couldn't have been all bad."

"Just because he painted flowers, you think he was a good guy?"

"Not exactly a good guy. Maybe he was just confused. Misguided."

"He caused the death of millions of people and you think he was just muddled in his thinking."

I was sorry I had opened the Pandora's Box. But I didn't like backing down in an argument. So I said nothing more. And Sylvia just walked away.

After I really pissed her off in that discussion about the nature of good and evil, I found myself realizing that I didn't want to lose her. So I wrote her a poem. (Yes, ladies and gentlemen of the jury, I write poetry on occasion.)

It was a good poem. Well, it was a flattering poem.

You'd think that a girl as smart as Sylvia with an IQ of 160 would see through it and think I was a bit of a fraud, that I was trying to make up with a flattering poem (which I refuse to share here). But she didn't.

She gave a great sigh and then hugged me and kissed me as only Sylvia could kiss. And one thing led to another.

Which made me rethink my life by the beach in New Zealand. Maybe if I wasn't alone and she was living with me, things would turn out okay. I discussed this option with her.

"Dixon," she said. "I'm sorry to inform you that I'm not going to move into some old shack with you on the shoreline of New Zealand. As you know, I want to go to Princeton. I'm going to study the human brain. I can't learn all there is about the human brain while living with you in New Zealand and growing—what was it?—cabbages? Cabbages are not that interesting."

"I probably shouldn't have told you about the cabbages," I said.

"Probably not."

"But I'm adrift. I need something more."

"You're just trying to fill a void in your life."

"Aren't we all?" I asked.

"Well, maybe your void is larger than my void and everybody else's void."

I know what you are thinking. Here is Dixon Carter. He is alone with a beautiful girl and they have just had some kind of physical and emotional intimacy (sorry, but you don't get more details than that, either) and why are they yammering about this void thing? But that's the sort of conversation we had.

"Dixon, Buddhists would argue that the void is a good thing. Empty your mind. Empty your thoughts. Free yourself from your attachment to your body and your desires. That is a good thing. Nirvana. Sunyata. True freedom and unification with the universe."

"I'm not ready to free myself of my desires," I countered.

"Then you have some work to do. Did you study for the European History test tomorrow?"

"No."

"Well, you should. It might help fill the void if the void is bothering you."

I thought I should just change the subject. "Did you like the poem?"

"I loved the poem. What inspired it?"

"You did," I said. It was the truth.

She smiled and kissed me again and then said, "Now you need to study for Euro History."

"Why?"

"Because maybe you should go to Princeton with me. We could both go there. I can study the human brain and you can study the human heart as revealed by the poets."

"Wow," I said. "Maybe I should."

I know how this all sounds to you. But this is the way we made up after an argument about good and evil or about anything else. Sylvia's dream was to go to Princeton and get a Ph.D. in neuroscience. I'm not entirely sold on post-secondary education, but then Princeton was where Einstein ended up. Maybe New Jersey has some kind of spiritual/intellectual vortex going. So maybe hanging around Princeton, New Jersey, for a few years is not a bad idea. Maybe something about the place would rub off on me.

It was also Einstein who said, "Any man who can drive safely while kissing a pretty girl is simply not giving the kiss the attention it deserves." I don't drive but I can see the point he's getting at. And kissing most definitely helps to fill the void.

DAY

FOUR

Memory and desire, stirring
Dull roots with spring rain

O kay, today is one of the good days. Not one of the dark ones.

The sun is out and bright. The wind is cool in my face. I am walking to school. I could take the bus but prefer to walk. By myself.

There is not a thing wrong with the world. It is perfect. I feel its perfection. I sing to it. I want to write poems to it. I want to feel the love of the trees, the sun, the birds. I hear traffic—tires kissing tarmac. That, too, is perfect.

I am thinking about Buddha, thinking about Einstein, thinking about how I can further enhance the beauty of this planet with my own skills.

Please understand that I am humble. I do not want to push my will on the world. I do not want to dismantle anything. I want to build—gently. I want to give back. I want my talents to be useful.

Compassion, kindness, and forgiveness—and to that, add tolerance.

All those words are mere abstractions. But actions always trump abstractions.

Last night I dreamed I was in a tunnel. I was crawling and going up a narrow passage where steps had been carved into the rocks. It seemed strangely Biblical. But well-lit, a kind of Disney Bible tunnel. I hit the end of the tunnel. A wall. And it was a message to retrace my steps and go back out into the world of daylight and possibility.

And so I did.

And woke up like this.

Euphoric.

Been down this path before, of course. I realize this is not "normal." But then I've never been normal. I remember that just yesterday, one of my many dark days, I felt like resigning from the human race. (Can a person do that?)

Today, I have no intentions of such things. I love humanity. I want to do whatever it takes to save us all from our own worst devices.

If I can save humanity, I can save myself. What do I mean by that? I mean I want to save myself from myself.

But let's not go there right now. Not on a day like this. No way.

The birds are singing. It feels good to be alive.

Evening now and a chance to recap the day.

My energy is fading and I feel sleep is not far off. Maybe another trip back into the tunnel. Maybe it will be Disney Biblical again. Or maybe not.

So you might be wondering, how does a euphoric sixteen-year-old cope with boring ole school on a day that God has created so righteous?

Truth is that it ain't that easy.

Thank God for Ms. Bartley's English class, though.

Ms. Bartley has seen my good days and my bad ones. I've made her classroom hell on some days and graced her with my more positive genius on others. She is a good soul, an old soul. And a patient one. Ms. Bartley was born to teach children who behave like angels and treat her like a goddess. Instead, she found herself at Wedgewood High School with classes filled with doodlers, texters, yawners, kids who ask questions about whether it is going to be on the test, and a small handful of keeners. And one brilliant but delicate bonehead like me who is an emotional ping-pong ball.

Ms. Bartley has the eyes of a saint and the heart of a poet.

Today the subject of the English class was Percy Bysshe Shelley. The poem, "To a Skylark."

Ms. Bartley (first name Evelyn) read the first stanza out loud:

Hail to thee, blithe spirit!
Bird thou never wert—
That from heaven, or near
Pourest thy full heart

In profuse strains of unpremeditated art.

Eyes rolled in unison around the room. I kept my gaze locked onto Ms. Bartley and when her own eyes looked my way, she knew I fully understood.

"Not all those words will be familiar to you, I know, but I wonder if anyone can express what it is the poet is feeling?"

I identified immediately with what old Shelley was feeling but I had long ago learned to tame myself and not burst into song, not jump on the Romantic poets' bandwagon and ride off into the heavens.

"What the frig is a wert?" Stein Levinson asked.

"It's just an old English way of saying 'were,'" Ms. B. said. "What else here? Blythe would mean happy. The skylark is so happy that he is pouring his happiness, his heart, into the sky with song—unpremeditated art."

"Freakin' birds don't have emotions," Stein countered.

I guess I couldn't restrain myself at that point. I jumped in without raising my hand. "But the poet is putting himself in the place of the bird. He sees the bird sing and feels this intense happiness within himself."

A large cloud of silence settled on the room.

I was used to it.

"Frig off," Stein said. But then Stein always said that.

When class was over, Ms. B. asked me to stay behind and sit with her while she ate her lunch. I said sure. She handed me half a sandwich across her desk and explained that it was avocado and cheese.

"You still write poetry?" she asked.

"Sometimes."

"I liked what you showed me. It seemed very honest."

"That's all I can be. Sometimes honesty isn't the best policy. But I'll stick with it. Hey, I liked the Shelley poem. Thanks for taking us there."

"Well, I think you might have been the only one who appreciated it. But what's with you today? You're all smiles."

"Oh, yeah. That. It's a good day."

Ms. B. nodded. She was a teacher who cared—I knew that. In a good way. Most of the other teachers just thought I was a pain in the ass. A smart ass. Crude, rude, and way too smart for his own good. Sometimes I was even hard on Ms. B.—for no good reason, other than the fact that I could turn against someone because of ... well, anything. One word. A look. Like I said, I'm tough to be around.

"Most days you hate school, right?"

I shrugged. "I think it's more than seventy percent of the time. But then I hit a day like this."

"Is it 'cause you're high?"

I smiled. Then laughed. Then took a bite into the avocado and cheese sandwich, which actually tasted a whole lot better than it sounded.

"Why is it that adults see a kid smiling too much and they figure he's on drugs?"

Ms. B. took a bite of her sandwich, wiped her mouth, and then said, "If it's some drug you're on, I'd like to try it myself." But I knew she was only joking.

Then she turned serious. "You think you're going to make it through the year this time?"

It was a dark note on what had been so far a very melodious day. But Ms. B. knew about last year. She knew about me.

"I don't know," I said. "I'm trying to stay off the meds. I think the good days are on the increase. But I'm not sure. I wish I could stand outside myself and observe me. Figure out how to keep me up. Not down."

"The Romantic poets—Keats, Shelley, Byron—they celebrated the extremes. When you were up, you were supposed to be really sky high—like that skylark. But when you were down, you were supposed to be really down.

> *But when the melancholic fit shall fall*
> *Sudden from heaven like a weeping cloud*
> *That fosters the droop-headed flowers all*
> *And hides the green hill in an April shroud.*

That's John Keats, 'Ode to Melancholy.' He's celebrating despair."

I didn't know what to say.

Ms. B. gave me a soft smile. A smile that said she thought she understood. A smile that said there was compassion in the world. But it was a sad smile, nonetheless. A smile that suggested she understood who I was and what I lived with.

And then I was back in the hallway, a bit more somber but still trying to hold onto the image of the sunlight from this morning when I had walked to school. And the happy sound of a world waking up—even my suburban world of cars and buses and traffic lights.

As I walked through the now-crowded hallways, I thought I could feel the presence of all the students who had walked through these halls in years past. I thought I could see them as phantoms—opening lockers, laughing, some serious, some hurting, some happy. And I felt so at home with them. I felt that I fit into *this* world, *this* school world of past, present, and even future. And therein was contentment. And joy.

DAY

FIVE

One must be so careful these days.

I'm still feeling fairly mellow but don't think it can last.

So Einstein said we can't solve our problems with the same thinking we used when we created them. Yeah, right on. Why didn't we elect Einstein the first president of the entire planet? Get a smart guy for once. Me? No, dude. I do not want to be the president of the planet. I don't think it is on my agenda.

Which brings up the issue: what is on my agenda?

That's a hard one, because I'm trying to sort out my ideas, my thoughts, my so-called illness, and my condition. I am, alas, a product of my culture, of my time, of my ancestry, and I'd prefer to step outside of all that.

And if I could step outside of all that conditioning, what would be left?

Me?

Or an empty shell. No content. No rug under my feet. No country. John Lennon said, imagine there's no countries. No heaven. No *thing* to believe in ... but everything. Yes.

And there was that poem I found floating around the Internet.

Check it out.

I'm Alive. I Believe in Everything.

Self. Brotherhood. God. Zeus. Communism.
Capitalism. Buddha. Vinyl records.
Baseball. Ink. Trees. Cures for disease.
Saltwater. Literature. Walking. Waking.
Arguments. Decisions. Ambiguity. Absolutes.
Presence. Absence. Positive and Negative.
Empathy. Apathy. Sympathy and entropy.
Verbs are necessary. So are nouns.
Empty skies. Dark vacuums of night.
Visions. Revisions. Innocence.
I've seen all the empty spaces yet to be filled.
I've heard all of the sounds that will collect
at the end of the world.
And the silence that follows.

I'm alive. I believe in everything.
I'm alive. I believe in it all.

Waves lapping on the shore.
Skies on fire at sunset.
Old men dancing in the streets.
Paradox and possibility.
Sense and sensibility.
Cold logic and half-truth.
Final steps and first impressions.
Fools and fine intelligence.
Chaos and clean horizons.
Vague notions and concrete certainty.
Optimism in the face of adversity.

I'm alive. I believe in everything.
I'm alive. I believe in it all.

Notice today's tone and flavor of me. I still have the edge, still unsettled, still searching. But not manic. Not down in the cave. In the light, instead. Head swollen with light. Surrounded by light. In another time, another spiritual domain, I may have believed myself to be some kind of savior, some spiritual healer. (Why not?)

But I have been trying to heal myself since childhood. On good days, I tell myself, I am strong, I can overcome the darkness within. And then. And then. I can muster my allies and forge out into the world to win hearts, win minds, win battles with no enemies other than myself.

We are our own worst enemies and, once that is understood, we do battle with ourselves through kindness and compassion.

All you have to do is love yourself, dude. No, really. Then you see how connected it all is. How loved we all are. We just need to learn how to wield that love like a soft, persuasive weapon that cannot be resisted.

Oh, if only Einstein were here with me now. "No problem can be solved from the same level of consciousness that created it," he said.

How does one make that leap? How do *I* make that leap?

Not easy to say, dude.

Not easy to say.

DAY

SIX

Your shadow at morning striding behind you
Or your shadow at evening rising to meet you

Well, you've probably been wondering about this "wasteland" business. So here are some thought variations on my personal notions of waste and such. Zeke's favorite word is, of course, "wasted." Two or three hits of Chowder House and he says he is wasted or blown or "nicely fucked up." He and I have, in fact, each been labeled a waster, which, if you look it up in the OED, means: *One who lives in idleness and extravagance; a squanderer or spendthrift.* Hah. Not us. Not me at all. And besides, as duly noted, I'm not really much of a drug taker, given my condition.

At night, I dip into that little poetry book Zekers

insisted I read—*The Waste Land and Other Poems.* Yes, "The Waste Land" by T.S. Eliot. Something you may have been forced to read in school. Very odd. Very much filled with obscure words and references. I don't really get it, but I keep going back to it like a puzzle that has to be solved. Which makes it just like me. A puzzle that needs to be solved. And I'm the only one who can do it.

(Oh, about my condition? Be patient, please. Let the story unfold in tangled tales and tributaries like this.)

So a land that was a "waste" or "wasteland" was one that was "uncultivated and uninhabited," which is not such a bad thing, is it? I suppose the notion is that it is uninhabitable. Meaning you and I can't live there because it is too hot or too dry or has unbreathable air.

And that brings us closer to the truth on several levels. I am, indeed, living in my own private wasteland—a land only I can inhabit, a land where maybe no one else could survive. Here, it gets lonely and cold, but also hot, and dark, and sometimes savagely bright. Sometimes the air is truly unbreathable and my thoughts are unthinkable. And it is all too much to live with.

And yet I take the next step forward into the wasteland and I survive. I survive because it is such a challenge. I survive in order to assert my will, to move forward—not toward salvation, but so I can go deeper into the uninhabitable region, deeper into the unknown.

Zeke introduced me to another poem by a guy named Randall Jarrell called "90 North" and in it, his protagonist goes deeper into the unknown to the top of the world and then states:

Turn as I please, my step is to the south.
The world—my world spins on this final point
of cold and wretchedness.

Reading that cheery bit along with my ole buddy Tough Shit Eliot is a real downer but it connects to something in me. It truly does. My vision of a ravaged inner landscape. Since those poems were written, though, our modern minds have been filled with multiple vivid visions of a post-apocalyptic world. Nuclear deserts and destroyed cities and vast ravaged landscapes and a world without hope. We live with these notions that we are not headed toward a brighter future but a bleaker one, an ultimate wasteland, either devoid of human beings or merely a stark setting for bone-chilling survival. These visions appear to me all the time in sleep and in waking. They come from deep within me and seem as real as you are real. I would take you there if I thought you could stand it. But you could not. So I keep the gates to my private wasteworld well locked and guarded by the hounds of my intellect.

But more of that later.

I told you this would not be easy.

Instead, let me tell you about my father.

My father was hoping to be a musical legend. He was a singer and lead guitar player in a band called Pegroot, and he's never been able to explain to me what that name means. His band was good and they were popular, and even produced one album with a song or two that played on radio stations, as he would say, "back in the day." They opened concerts for big names you would recognize and seemed to be on the road to success. But their bass player got killed in a motorcycle accident and the new bass player somehow brought "bad vibes" into the music. And it wasn't just that. As my father said, "Everything just changed." The music business, the audiences, the way music was recorded, the way it was sold. Nothing was the same anymore. And it was clear the band had hit a plateau, and then Pegroot began its descent into mediocrity, obscurity, and poverty.

So my dad, Archibald—or Archie as he preferred—did the unthinkable. He hung up his Fender Strat. He cut his hair. He went to law school. He got his papers. He met my mother and married her in a church. He took a job in a law firm—Struthers and Struthers—and he defended drunk drivers in court, sought out injury cases for lawsuits, and handled divorces. He did some criminal stuff—even defended a murderer once. He knew the creep was guilty but defended the lout, got him off, and the man murdered again. My father never touched a case of violence again. He told me this story one night when I was young, a long time ago, when the two of us were alone in the car driving home from a movie.

And why am I telling you this?

I am telling you this so you can begin to understand some things about me. It is not just ego, my friend. It is just that I live in both joy and turmoil, and if I am to survive the darker days, it will be because I can communicate what and who I am and where I came from and where I am. And if you will follow me and say truthfully, at the end of this tale, that you understand me, then, just maybe, I can save myself.

So the guitar sits idle in its case and it has been replaced by law books, and my father's long bushy hair is now much shorter, much thinner. And he has an offspring who shares my name and sits fidgeting in European History class, thinking about Einstein and even Winston Churchill, and envisioning Vincent Van Gogh's starry night (or *de sterrennacht*, as he would say in Dutch) painting.

I should bring Sylvia back into this story.

Sylvia saw me losing it today in school. My knees were shaking. I was sweating. The wasteland was looming all around me in math, and I walked out of class without permission. Sylvia followed.

"What is it?" she asked.

"Everything," I said.

"It will be okay," she said and took my hand and walked me out of the dark hallways into sunlight. "Are you taking your meds?"

"No," I said. "They make me feel dead to the world."

"But this is bad ... the way you feel now."

"I need to feel this," I said.

"Why?"

"Because this is real."

"I understand."

Language failed to take me beyond what I had said so I fell into a silent place. And Sylvia held my hand and we walked until we came to a field that was all brown with winter, and a single tree that looked stark and dead, and yet that, too, was only winter. But the tree was lit up from behind with sunlight through its bare limbs and, as we approached, a thousand starlings launched from those bare branches and the cold hard world was filled with the sound of wings and the vision of flying birds.

And I knew I could make it through another day.

DAY

SEVEN

In the mountains, there you are free.

Day seven without the meds. No sodium valproate. No lithium carbonate. Just my own body producing the chemicals I need to live, to think. My own brain dishing out dopamine and serotonin and all the rest.

Did you know Churchill was bi-polar? Winston Fucking Churchill and he got England through the war with Hitler. He was the one who said, "Never, never, never give up." He also wisely said, "If you are going through hell, keep going." His drug of choice was alcohol and, apparently, this is part of what got him through the war. Sheer will, determination, and a bit of booze. Who could fault the man?

So where am I now? A place of clarity. The anger has dissipated. The birds are singing. I am sitting on a bench in the park, kissing Sylvia. Sylvia likes to be kissed and I like kissing her. Today I am not going through hell but there is a relationship, is there not, between what we refer to as heaven and the existence of hell? In the old days, religion found it easier to show evidence of the devil than of God, so if you could prove the devil existed, then it must be true (they argued) that God existed. If you could prove hell, then heaven.

My moment here with Sylvia is as close to euphoria, as close to heaven, as I can imagine.

My religion does not insist that hell is just around the corner. But maybe it is. I've been there before, remember. I have a vivid map in my brain. I know the pathway there. I know how to recognize the markers and the destination. I have been there and Winston was right. When you are going through it, just keep going.

But not today, my seventh day without meds.

Let's talk about what it means to be "different." If you are reading this, you are probably one of us—one of my tribe. Not just my unique tribe of upper/downer-ites. Just someone who knows your brain does not operate like the brains of so-called normal people. (But then, normal people are so tedious and boring, are they not?) When was it, exactly, that you figured out you were odd/weird/unique/peculiar/singular?

Probably when you started school, if you hadn't figured it out earlier. I had no brother or sister to call me weird/retarded/warped/fucked up or whatever. And my parents were kind. When I was five years old, my father had a look on his face when I asked him odd questions. His curious look said that my question was way out there and he was wondering why I was asking such bizarre stuff.

Questions like:

Who is the president of the universe?

Who owns the moon?

How can I grow wings?

How old is gravity?

Where do ideas come from?

How can I invent happiness for everyone?

And so on.

My father had that look that said: *How did this strange kid get to be my son?* (My father, nice guy that he is, is, alas, a card-carrying, fully-registered normal person.) His look also said that he loved me for who I was, weirdness and curiosity and all. But as I grew older, I also realized that there had been pity in that look. Something that said: *My kid is gonna be a strange one. He will not ever have it easy or fit in.* And, of course, the pity in his eyes grew out of the love in his heart.

So he'd answer something like this:

"You are the president of the universe. I elected you."

"You and I own the moon, but we're willing to share it with others."

"Growing wings is easy. You just need to eat a lot of vegetables and fruit and tap your shoulder blades ten times each, every day."

"Gravity has only been around since I was a kid. Everyone

thought it was a good idea to keep things from flying off into space, but I'm not sure it's always a good thing."

"Ideas are gifts from certain invisible birds."

"The way you can invent happiness for everyone is to just smile. You have a wonderful smile and it will work every time. But the result will only be temporary, so you'll have to smile a lot."

So, in retrospect, maybe my dad had been one of the odd ones, too, at one point. Maybe he could still tap into that unique world. Maybe he was like that when he was in Pegroot. Or maybe he took drugs. But he kept that side of himself covered up most times. After all, he was a lawyer (not a guitarist in a rock band) who handled drunk-driving cases and divorce settlements and small-time criminals who had stolen cars and wallets. Drunk drivers and unhappy couples and thieves didn't usually want to talk to my dad about gravity or the moon or even happiness.

I guess I didn't really clue into what was different about me (what was wrong with me, you might say) until I started school.

Then it became crystal clear.

I felt all alone in school. Kids seemed to have a natural way of running around together, bumping into each other, and laughing—getting to know each other easily. They shared lunches, threw rocks, kicked balls, and all that stuff. But not me. I was the kid staring at an ant crawling up the brick wall of the school. I was content with the ant and didn't need all those confusing, noisy kids.

For some reason, staring at ants made some kids dislike me. I won't bore you with all the details but it turned out that there were always certain kids—even right up through high school—who had an almost innate dislike for me because of the way I was. There were many labels.

But I can't say I brought on the wrath of my dim-witted classmates (yeah, most all those innate haters of me were not so smart) on purpose. Not until I turned fifteen. By then I had this chip you've noticed on my shoulder. And I knew how to get them riled. And I liked it. Even if it meant a punch in the head (for me) sometimes.

You are wondering why I have not said much about my mother.

My mother was never, ever what you could call normal. She was an intense person who sometimes danced around the house, who made tasks like washing dishes or cleaning the floor seem like pure joy. She liked to play games with me outside and take me on hikes and show me flowers and leaves and insects—and she was always naming things. Always insisting I know the proper names of things: pin oak, calendula, Queen Anne's lace, mosquito larvae, red-tailed hawk. She knew the names of everything natural or man-made. She kept lists that I would see sometimes. In a journal she showed me, she had chapters with tree names, bug names, car names, appliance manufacturers, movie stars, constellations, baseball players, and rock bands. At the top of the rock band page was the word: Pegroot.

There were no other notes. Just names. It was like she wanted to catalogue everything. And she always kept the journal handy to add new items in the proper chapter at whatever time of day. But if she misplaced the journal, she got very, very upset, and sometimes my father would have to come home from work to help her calm down and find it.

Mostly, all the naming was a happy thing to share with me when I was little. But sometimes she'd look at a flower and not be able to remember its name and she'd start to get angry. Other things made her angry: stuff being out of place in the kitchen, or me making a mess in the living room, or cutting up her magazines to make collages of my own. I was a huge fan of glue and scissors and pictures, but often I did make a crazy mess of things. And she'd get mad at me.

She never hit me. But things got pretty dark.

So, you are starting to think there is inherited weirdness here, thanks to my mother. And that may be true but it may also be wrong. I don't know how my mother got through her school years with all the labeling and need for order, since the world is such a cluttered and disorderly place. She either held back or it didn't kick in until she was older.

A couple of years ago, when I tried to discuss this with my father, his face went kind of rigid and he looked away, then admitted, "Your mother didn't start to ... change ... until after you were born."

Oh.

He didn't mean to, but my brain locked onto the fact

that something about my once potentially normal mother changed because of me.

Good old Dad added, "Maybe it was something hormonal. That's what one doctor said."

She had her good days and her bad. It was maybe 80/20 at first and then 70/30 and then 50/50. Fifty/fifty pretty well sent her to see the psychiatrist, and the psychiatrist put her on some kind of medication.

And the first thing she did was burn her book of lists. I came home from school and she was burning it in our living room fireplace and cooking a hotdog on a fork over the flame. She was crying. And I sat with her and cried, too. And she said she loved me. When I told my father what she had done, he smiled in a sad sort of way and said, "Well, your mother always really liked hotdogs."

She settled down after that. No more 50/50. It was pretty "normal" around my house, but it felt like another type of fire had gone out in her. She was just going through the motions of the day-to-day and my father was plenty sad about the change, but he always tried to put a good spin on it.

This change in my mom threw me into my own dark place, and that sent me to see the same psychiatrist. He thought I was just a normal teenage kid at first and gave me a pep talk about my mother but asked me to keep coming back.

During an appointment one day, however, I was feeling that I could do anything. I felt that all I had to do was finish high school and go out into the world and start fixing everything. I mean everything that was wrong with it. I wanted to be a rock singer like my dad. I wanted to write beautiful poems. I wanted to make love to beautiful women. I wanted to cure diseases. I would make millions of dollars and give it away. I would travel the world. I would write novels. I would study everything about the human brain and human heart. I would bring happiness to people who thought they never could be happy.

And, I guess, I was kind of worked up. My eyes were wide. I was sweating. I was so excited. It wasn't like a daydream that I could do these things. It was like knowing for a fact that I *would do these things*.

Doc didn't exactly get what I was saying. His face said this was serious business. He was writing some notes. "How do you know you can do these things?" he asked. But the frown on his face said it all.

This psychiatrist had been one of the other tribe—he'd been like the kids on the playground way back there who saw me studying the ant on the school wall. One of the ones who had labels for me that were not kind. One of the ones who wanted to tell the world: *There's something wrong with this one. This kid is really flaky. This kid is pretty fucked up.*

Like mother, like son. I, too, was supposed to start taking medication. I did not have what my mother had. There were different labels. I don't like those labels, but once they are sewn into your shirt, it's hard to get rid of them.

And I now had mine.

And when the meds kicked in, I knew that none of that

stuff, that glorious stuff I had said in the shrink's office, was ever going to come true.

And that made me angry.

DAY

EIGHT

April is the cruellest month, breeding
Lilacs out of the dead land

Today, alone in my room, I was reading Eliot again. The poem disturbed me. Full of ugliness, despair, and rats and dead bodies. It's not April but it's late winter—a gloomy, moody thing of a month, and something has been building inside me. They could all see it. My father asked what was wrong. Sylvia said I was kissing strangely as if I was attempting to kiss her by remote control from another planet. Zeke said I was acting antsy, but it was Zeke who was always antsy, pumped up as usual on glucose, caffeine, and taurine—and God knows what went into those energy drinks. Zeke said he had met the perfect girl for him, though it wasn't a girl at all but one of our classmates' mothers, and

I said that was not cool, not cool at all. And it disturbed me.

I couldn't find FWD for some soothing advice because Dave was always chilled, always telling me to tone down and not get flustered, not to take the material world so seriously, not to get rattled by a damn thing. But some guys at the beach said Fairweather had gone to Australia for the week. Which seemed not quite right because I thought that he had given away most of his money or something. (Dave never wanted to talk about his once-upon-a-time fortune and that surfwear empire he founded). But the word among the surfers was that he was at Bells Beach down under, getting tubed in emerald green water. Yeah, I could have used a dose of Dave's mellow mindset, but he had flown and he was far, far away.

So what was happening to me was what had been labeled the "kindling effect." One stressful thing after another. (Isn't that the definition of life, dude?)

Like a fool, I had chosen fucking T.S. Eliot and his damned "Waste Land" poem to write an essay on for Ms. Bartley. And there were lilacs in the second line. The lilacs, I knew, came from one of my mother's list of shrubs—a purple flowering shrub.

In Greek mythology, Pan, the horny god of the forest, chased some girl named Syringa and, in order for her to elude him, she changed herself into the sweet-smelling flowery bush—what we call lilacs. They bloom early in the spring, even during the wet and dreary and cold springs we have here. But Eliot's lilacs bloom out of the "dead land" and I was haunted by that dead land. It reminded me of what the meds had done to me and why I would not go back there. The lilacs of my imagination had bloomed once I left the drugs and the dead land and came back to the euphoric world of Dixon Carter, boy genius, hope of civilization, and poet of the future.

The poem seemed to be emphatically telling me that Eliot was one of my tribe, though, and his vision was a dark one. I thought I was brave enough, strong enough for such dark journeys, and if I could have perhaps kept it inside that little book, I might have been okay.

But my mom was acting funny—distant and lost and not the mom she had once been, now that the lists were all gone and the house was not as organized or tidy.

And no FWD to calm me. And there I was, afraid I might lose Sylvia because I was kissing her from another planet. And Zeke right now just seemed to have his own agenda, which involved skateboarding, his new passion for another high-energy drink called Fire, and an obsessive interest in somebody's mother. And my dad was a bit too much caught up in work—trying to untangle two partners in a toy manufacturing business who were suing each other over breach of contract.

And then this thing happened in school. I had not had a face-to-face with the Enemy for a while.

Lance had been a fairly unobtrusive but obnoxious kid through much of his school career. He had been overweight and dull and tried to draw attention to himself by farting in clever ways in Grade 6 and by eating anyone's leftover food in the cafeteria. But, in the last year or so, he had stopped farting in such a public way, started eating only the food his mother packed for him. He trimmed down, got taller and strangely meaner, and was now like a hunter on the prowl for new prey each new day.

I had watched Lance blossom into this monster and, for a while, tried to simply stay out of his way. When he neared, Zeke would say, "Shields up," and we'd walk the other way and not give eye contact. But then on this particular day when I was feeling on edge, there he was, the new improved, meaner, leaner Lance, talking to Sylvia. I tried to get Sylvia's attention and she tried to shoo me away. She knew Lance would zero in on me. But I didn't shoo easily. And although I knew Sylvia would never go for a guy like Lance, I was jealous. Sylvia was my mix of "memory and desire," my girl, my love, my anchor in a world both intellectual and sensuous.

So I walked up and blurted out, "Fuck off," in such a matter-of-fact, no-nonsense, casual way that Lance had to ask, "Excuse me?" So I repeated it in Italian: "*Vaffanculo.*"

It appeared that he didn't know Italian (and you'll have to bear with me and understand that one of my hobbies is to learn profanity in many foreign languages). So I tried Japanese: "*Kuso kurae,*" which literally means "eat shit," but if he were to have comprehended, it would have meant more or less the same. I tried Mandarin: "*Goon kai,*" then Welsh: "*Chacahu bant,*" even Kazakh: "*Zaibal,*" and finally Latin: "*Efutue.*"

Lance just stared down at me with his mouth open as if unable to say something in any language, since none would be able to express his profound confusion melded with his outrage. Keep in mind: Lance had been storing up this rage for over a decade, hoarding insults and jokes hurled his way by our classmates.

Sylvia grabbed my arm and tried to walk me away. She knew what I had been saying in my crude multilingual and oh-so-bloody-stupido way.

"No, you fuck off," Lance finally sprayed. But I knew it wouldn't end there. He grabbed my head from behind and planted my face firmly into the wall, in a deft, precise way that seemed to have been well rehearsed. Sylvia shrieked in a manner I had never heard her shriek. Others stared. There was a display of blood on my part. Lance wanted to prove some kind of point, of course.

"Freak," he said, addressing me as I crumpled to the floor.

I felt pain and I felt anger. And the worst thing about that is that it felt good. And all I could remember was one more version of the quintessential phrase. In German, I looked up at the Enemy and announced: "*Verpiss dich.*" Perhaps Lance somehow understood German, or at least the inflection of the words, because his response was a strong nonverbal but syntactically appropriate kick to my groin.

It had been quite the scene and I had made my point, I think (although it was indeed a pointless point), and endured the response. And Lance walked away lest he get in trouble with the authorities at school. And I did not go over into the dark just then. I recovered. But I knew something was not quite right.

"I will show you fear in a handful of dust," says the poet.

DAY

NINE

There is shadow under this red rock.

We all need anchors in our lives to keep us from drifting off into oblivion. I was a swimmer in the waters of Lethe off and on throughout my life, and lifesavers had been thrown my way more than once. Zeke had often been the one to see me drowning and try to bring me back to the shores of reason and calm, although the beaches were always of rough stone and large, impervious rock.

And so Zeke deserves to be canonized herein before the story proceeds.

Zeke was always smarter than any of his teachers would guess. He was more sensitive than he appeared. He, seemingly the most proud weed-whacked of teenage skate dogs, had his smokescreen intact. He had his cover. No one ever expects Zeke to be dependable, intellectual, or deep. But he is all three.

He had mastered the art of growing gonzo grass in his closet with aluminum foil walls, humidifier, and grow lights. He had it down to a science, and I do believe his claim that his Chowder House breed was his very own ultimate hybrid—"Easy on your head, not a body stone, but a spiritual cleanser and intellectual enhancer."

I myself was afraid to smoke too much of it. I knew that some people who smoked weed could have a psychotic reaction or even experience what is known as "depersonalization." And believe me, as a certified textbook, psychologically fragile person, I was familiar with both zones. But I was Zeke's friend and would keep him company when he communed with the Chowder gods.

Zeke came from a funny family. His dad died soon after he was born. His mom remarried a marble sculptor named Brian. As you might guess, not many marble sculptors in the twenty-first century make much of a living, but Brian had melded his craft with the "money-making death machine," as he called it. He had offered his services to funeral homes and privately owned cemeteries, so he created rather elegant small monuments to be placed on gravesites. A national magazine article about him made him very popular among the grieving hordes and he had more business than he could handle.

Sadly, Brian was so caught up with the death machine art that he was ignoring Zeke's mother and she left him—and Zeke, as it turned out—to move in with an Oriental carpet importer. Brian may or may not have known about the Chowder House closet op, but if he did, he never said a word. He might have clued into something when Zeke asked for a pure marble hash pipe for Christmas, but Brian just went along and made him the heaviest, most elegant white hash pipe the world had ever known. The marble came from the same quarry in Italy where Michelangelo had once found the perfect stone he needed for the statue of David.

Perhaps this is more than you need to know.

Still, I'm hoping you can hear this out.

Because Zeke is one of a kind.

Zeke had a pet tarantula named Aldous Huxley and he took very good care of it. Sadly, this breed of creature—a rose-haired tarantula—only lives for four or five years and Aldous died, presumably of old age. Zeke cried as we buried him in his backyard and erected the small black marble monument. "It's a sad thing to have to outlive your pet," Zeke said.

Zeke was always a bit of a teenage gawker of girls and women, which probably makes him less likely for any nominations of sainthood, but he never actually said crude things about the objects of his attention. And he confessed to me that one of his true dreams was to find the "right girl." One who he could settle down with by the time he hit twenty. "She would be beautiful and I would be brilliant and we'd have a really sweet homemade half-pipe in the backyard, a greenhouse where we'd grow organic vegetables and buzz, a nice backyard with a Slip 'n' Slide for our two kids. We'd get old together and I'd invent this device for helping to stem the tide of violence."

And, of course, Zeke is a great proponent of nonviolent everything. One of his classic lines is: "If only we could wage a nonviolent war." He doesn't think war could be eradicated, so, instead, it would have to be a peaceful war. "It's all about the paradoxes," Zeke said. "Embrace the paradox and you can master the universe."

The aforementioned device is something that would electronically alter brainwave activity so that it quells anger and therefore violence. He said, "It's all about alpha waves and beta waves and directing the right UHF pulse to the right part of the brain." He swore it could be done but worried that, if the gun lobby found out, they would try to kill him. "And that wouldn't be fair to my wife and kids," he said. Which were, of course, hypothetical, but then so was the device.

Zeke and Dave are often on the same wavelength, as you might guess, and both have been a positive influence on yours truly as I reach for the heavens on my good days and plummet to the hard unforgiving earth on others.

Aside from the death of his first dad and the exodus of his mother on her magic carpet ride, Zeke floats through life when he isn't skating down at the park or trying to achieve flight while skidding down metal railings. He is a B minus student. He doesn't like C's and, if he found himself getting the occasional A minus or B, he'd cut back so that the world did not start to have higher expectations of him. "It's the B minus students who will ultimately save humanity," he said.

I won't even start to try to explain the logic of that, but Zeke had his reasons. "People who strive too much always fuck up everything."

"Chill," is one of Zeke's favorite words.

As you can see, Zeke is one of a kind. He was not manufactured like many of us are by parents and teachers and television and Internet. He is what they used to call a "self-made man" at sixteen. He has a license to be his own dude, and his homage to the rest of society is simply to achieve a B minus in the appropriate institutions of childhood and remain aloof from destructive influences of education and mass media that would in any way alter him.

"Red Bull is my only vice," he sometimes says. (Not the weed, of course, since that was a sacrament in the cathedrals of Zekedom.) "It's part of the paradox," he admitted. "A highly commercialized caffeine drink is the opposite of chill, the antithesis of natural."

Zeke had volunteered to go to New Zealand with me and grow cabbages if I needed him. "But we'll have to find some really sweet New Zealand chicks," he said. "I hear they can be really mellow."

Well, my New Zealand dreams vanished when I realized Sylvia wouldn't want to go there with me and I wasn't ready to go to a far-off island nation without her. But Zeke had already gone to an online dating site and made friends with a girl named Lacey who lived on a sheep farm at a legendary surf town called Raglan. It turned into a really romantic and—if you believe Zeke—torrid love affair via Skype. I told him I didn't want to know any of the details of how that could work and he kept that part to himself.

Well, by now you're wondering why I'm going on so long about Zeke rather than myself.

But I need this, okay. I need to go down this path and you will see why.

Zeke has never had a professional haircut in his life. He asked Brian to cut his hair and Brian applied certain stone-sculpting principles, I think, to cutting his stepson's hair, so it was always unique and interesting. What Zeke called "the asymmetric look." And he bragged about it. But he is not otherwise terribly concerned about his appearance. Torn jeans, long-sleeve T-shirts with the name of obscure indie bands on them, and those curious sculpted haircuts.

And I guess I now have to tell you what happened today because it will get to the heart of who Zeke is.

We were walking along the bank of the river after school. It was winter and the river was frozen. It was cold and we were watching our breath make interesting little clouds. Zeke had a can of the Bull in his hand but, just for the record, he had not visited the Chowder House. We were, as they say, minding our own business.

Up ahead was an old woman wearing what appeared to be an oversize man's winter coat, pajama pants, and knee-high rubber boots. She was yelling frantically at something out on the ice. The something she was yelling at was a dog, a galloping yellow Lab chasing a tennis ball that someone must have thrown out onto the ice. "Gus," she yelled. "Gus, you stupid idiot dog! Get back here!"

Gus had just then snatched the rolling tennis ball and was skidding to a stop on the ice. People on shore were watching. We were all thinking the same thing. The woman kept yelling at her dog to come back. He had slipped to a stop spread-eagled and was just beginning to turn back when he stumbled and fell.

And then the ice cracked. And, yes, the dog was in the water. The woman let out an ear-piercing scream. Along with other onlookers, we watched in horror as the Lab tried to pull itself up onto the ice with its front paws, the damn tennis ball still in its mouth.

Zeke and I had arrived at where the old woman was standing and she looked at us. Her face was frozen in fear. "Help us," she said.

A strange sort of calm came over Zeke as he handed me his cell phone and the can of Red Bull and said, "Call 9-1-1," and at first I didn't know why he was asking me to make the call. But I dutifully punched in 9-1-1.

When I looked up, Zeke had dropped down over the embankment and was slowly walking out on the ice. At once the ice began to crack and moan. The dog continued its frantic effort to get up out of the icy water.

After a few steps, Zeke was down on his knees and, a bit further along, he was on his belly pulling himself forward with his fingernails on the now undulating ice.

When he reached the dog, he threw an arm forward and grabbed the dog's collar. At first he couldn't pull the dog out of the water. Instead, it looked like he was sliding forward himself, ready to fall into the icy bath. But as Zeke struggled to raise the mutt, the dog got one back foot on the ice and suddenly almost leapt up out of the water. Once on the ice, the dog comically shook itself the way dogs do and ran toward shore and the old lady, who was calling it by name over and over, "Gus, Gus, Gus, Gus!" The dog still had the tennis ball in its mouth.

I heard a siren somewhere in the distance. Zeke lay still on the ice, not moving, and I could tell he was breathing hard because I could see his breath, and his body was heaving up and down. I yelled to him to turn around and move. Not raising himself up, he slowly began to shift his body around until he was facing shore. I yelled some more.

Zeke waved at me and, like an idiot, he smiled. Then he did not move for several long seconds as he tried to catch his breath.

And then he began to push himself forward on his belly back toward shore. But he was having a hard time getting a grip. His fingers must have been freezing at that point. When he tried to raise himself on his hands and knees, I saw the smile fade. On shore, as the old woman was hugging and chastising her wet dog, we all heard the sound. It was like a distant muffled cannon going off.

The ice gave way and Zeke was in the water. Worse yet, as he slipped into the water, he grabbed for the ice ahead of him and it kept breaking. When he did get a hold, his hands kept slipping off and his body kept dipping back down into the river. He was in big trouble. And now that the water was open, I could see there was a strong current wanting to pull him under the ice.

At first I didn't move. I was squeezing the phone held in my hand. I began to dial 9-1-1 again, but stopped, threw the phone on the ground, and walked forward. I was scared out of my mind. I did not want to go out there. I slowly eased myself over the embankment and was kneeling on the snow-crusted ice by the shore. I, too, went down on all fours and began to crawl.

I took a few tentative moves forward and felt the ice already soft and uncertain beneath my hands. I looked up and saw Zeke clawing at the ice, still unable to get a grip. I knew he would not be able to pull himself back up. Each frantic attempt looked weaker than before. I thought about that current that would not just pull him down but pull him under the river ice as it raced to the sea.

I watched in horror as he went under once but popped back up. Then a second time.

I did not see the men rushing toward the river behind me.

I didn't know what was going on when someone grabbed my feet roughly and started pulling me backwards. I was about to scream when I saw other rescuers in orange rescue suits scurrying out onto the ice—three of them tied together with rope, lying flat, moving forward on their stomachs, some kind of claws attached to their hands. In seconds, the first man reached the water and, just as Zeke was going down again, he dropped into the river and put two arms around my freezing buddy.

The other rescuers had a hard time getting the two of them

out of the water. The ice bent under the weight, collapsed, and broke, but now other men on shore were tugging the rescue line. The man who had pulled me roughly back to shore asked if I was okay, and I nodded. We watched as the rescuer and rescued were dragged back to shore through the collapsing ice.

I stumbled up the embankment and walked with the men as they led an ashen-white, nearly unconscious Zeke toward a waiting ambulance. The old woman, tears rolling down her face, was shrieking at him, "Thank you! Thank you! Thank you!"

Without asking, I got in the ambulance with my good friend.

The siren sounded and the ambulance sped off. Zeke, covered in blankets and with a paramedic hovering over him, turned to me and smiled.

"Good one," I said. "You done good."

Zeke was gasping. "Did you see me go under?"

I nodded.

"I went under three times. I thought I'd lost it the last time."

"I know. I was watching. What was going through your head?"

He shook his head. "I don't know what I was thinking about. I was in a panic, but then came some strange kind of calm. I wasn't cold then or anything. And I think I saw something."

Leave it to Zeke to get weird on me at a time like this. "What did you see?"

The paramedic had stopped hovering and was leaning up, waiting to see what the answer would be.

Zeke just smiled a big shit-eating smile and said, "Everything, man. Everything."

DAY

NINE—CONTINUED

O you who turn the wheel and look to windward

The hospital phoned Zeke's house but no one answered. His attending doctor was suggesting he stay in the hospital overnight, but he insisted he was totally fine and ready to go home. He did seem perfectly okay and the doc admitted that all his vital signs were as good as could be. Eventually, after that doc brought in a second doc to check him over, they agreed Zeke was totally okay, except they made him promise to go to his own doctor the next day for a check-up. All the docs agreed Zeke had just the kind of heart and lungs they liked to see: strong and steady.

So we took a cab to Zeke's house and he paid the driver with a soggy twenty-dollar bill.

When we got there, we found Brian in his studio. Brian

was using some kind of grinder on a piece of stone that looked like it might eventually be a large kitten. The rock he was working on was what I had learned was alabaster—or, as Zeke referred to it, "alabastard rock." There was white dust everywhere, coating everything in the room, including Brian who looked like he'd been doused with talcum powder. When he took off his glasses, he smiled. "Wow, what have you guys been up to?" Zeke had on loaner clothes from the hospital that made him look a bit like someone who gets A's in high school math classes.

Zeke told the story as if it had happened to someone else, and then he gave that goofy smile and shrugged.

"Holy shit," Brian said, rubbing some of the white rock powder from his cheek. And then he gave Zeke a hug.

We hung out for a bit in Zeke's bedroom where he showed me how well the marijuana plant was doing in his closet. It was nearly three feet tall and full of buds. "Isn't it beautiful?" he said.

I admitted it was. I loved the green of the five-part leaves and the pungent earthy aroma.

Zeke said he didn't want to smoke but he'd give me some CH if I wanted any. I politely declined. Truth is, he looked kind of buzzed. Something was going through his head.

"Now can you tell me what happened when you were under?"

The Zekester just kept shaking his head sideways. "I can try."

I waited as he inhaled oxygen just like he was taking a hit from a joint.

"Well, I felt the cold and, at first, it was like sharp knives stabbing at every part of my body. All I felt was panic as my fingernails kept losing their grip on the ice. Then I was under and my lungs felt like they were on fire. I felt the current tugging. I kept fighting it, fighting everything."

Zeke took another hit of bedroom air. "Well, a million images went racing through my head—I'm still trying to process that. Some were like scenes from my life. Like you and me down at the skate park on that one special summer night. But there was much more. People I knew and people I didn't recognize—and then it just kept going. It was too much to figure out, and I guess I thought I must be dying and this is what it's like, but that didn't seem to scare me much 'cause I had stopped struggling."

"In the ambulance you said you saw 'everything.' What did you mean?"

He nodded yes now. "That's what it felt like. I was seeing—no, not just seeing, I was ... um ... feeling, experiencing everything. I don't know how that can be, but what if we have the capacity to do just that and we just can't tap into our ability to do it until ..."

He paused and looked around his room as if looking for some assistance to help him finish what he was saying.

Another deep long pull on the pungent air. He looked me straight in the eye and finished the sentence. "Until we are about to die?" He had tears in his eyes now.

I waited, said nothing. Yeah, he'd been that close. "You saved that lady's dog, dude. You deserve some kind of medal."

"Fuck the medal," Zeke said smiling. "I got to experience ..." He threw his arms out wide as if to embrace the world. "I got to experience everything. And it was fucking amazing. I'm still trying to digest it. But it's fading away. I was hanging onto it, but now it's slipping. Man, I don't want to lose this."

He suddenly looked serious. "Shit, I am losing those images. But now I can remember one of the last things going through my head. It didn't seem so bad at the time but now ..." He trailed off again.

"What?"

"No. I'm not going there."

"Okay. So just tell me what it felt like when you were pulled from the water."

"They say things go black when you were where I was. But it never went black. It was always bright. My eyes were closed and it was illuminated by something in there, wherever that was. And I had just been delivered all this crazy, amazing, powerful stuff, and then—wham. I felt that guy's arms wrap around me just then and he was pulling me roughly up and onto the collapsing ice. I felt a chunk of it graze along my cheek and it hurt. And then my lungs were exploding and my head was exploding. And I guess I wanted to go back to where I had just been. How crazy is that? And then I was in the ambulance with you, Dixon."

Brian knocked on the door. "You two soldiers want a Red Bull?"

Zeke smiled and let out a big puff of air like he'd been holding his breath. "Sure thing."

At the kitchen table, Brian used a wet cloth to wipe the alabaster dust off his face. "We should call your mother," he said.

"Nah," Zeke insisted. "I don't want to go there now. She'd give me a lecture. Maybe it was a stupid thing I did."

"You should have called for help," Brian said. "You shouldn't have gone out on the ice." He paused. "But you did what you did and now you're okay."

There was an awkward silence as Brian sipped his coffee and Zeke and I downed some of the Bull.

"But you know what's funny?" Brian added. "I'm home here sculpting a stone for someone whose cat has died and is buried in a pet cemetery, and you're out saving a golden Lab. Maybe I lost out on more work, thanks to you." It was meant to be a joke, but as soon as he'd said it, Brian knew it was a lame one.

INTERLUDE

I stopped writing in my journal after that day. It seemed pretty pointless. Everything seemed pointless and meaningless. It was a long time before I could pick up the thread and finish the story. I almost didn't finish it. You'll understand why.

CHAPTER

ONE

Looking into the heart of light, the silence

Word got out around school the next day about what happened the previous afternoon.

And you know what? Nobody seemed to give a shit. Yeah. Well, Sylvia gave us both a hug, but beyond that, nada. Everybody else, I think, was so caught up in their own pissy little lives with their own pissy little concerns that, well, it just didn't matter to them.

I was a little disappointed in my own lame performance that afternoon by the river. Whatever I had done was half-assed, and I don't think I would have done what Zeke did, but then he was always a bit more impetuous than me. And he had the scars to prove it. Now he had this notch on his belt.

I figured it was just me. This gnawing feeling in my gut. Figured I just didn't know how to make sense of what Zeke had told me about his near-death thing. Or maybe I was just still scared that we both could have drowned that day. What if the rescue squad had been five minutes later? Yeah, what if? What if a lot of things?

I was beginning to sense the spiral. It had an initial taste, an indefinable sound. A smell, even. I'd been there before. I knew.

But I was much stronger now. As the dark clouds began to form during European History class, I fought it. I'd been off the meds for ten days. I was that strong, I told myself. But there seemed no end to the wars in Europe.

I stared at the blackboard list that Mr. Schmoll had created during his lunch hour. It didn't make sense that Europe, like almost anywhere else on earth, had an endless parade of warfare. And this was only part of the list of twentieth-century wars.

1910 Albanian Revolt
1911–1912 Italian–Turkish War
1912–1913 First Balkan War
1913 Second Balkan War
1914 Albanian Peasant Revolt
1914–1918 World War I
1917–1921 Russian Civil War
1917–1921 Soviet–Ukrainian War
1918 Georgian–Armenian War
1918 Turkish–Georgian War
1918 Finnish Civil War

I was thinking about Zeke's imaginary device and about his "nonviolent war." I looked over to where he sat by the window and I could see that his head was down and he was asleep. Probably reliving those visions he had described as he dreamed. Mr. Schmoll was oblivious, as usual, to whether anyone was paying attention to him or not, as he rattled off the names of war after war and a less than colorful description of each one. When the bell rang, I bolted over to Zeke and shook him gently until he lifted his head.

"Where am I?" he asked.

"European History. You just missed a bunch of wars of the early twentieth century."

"Aw, shucks," he said, and wearily lifted himself up. But as he was rising, he suddenly fell back into his seat.

"What?" I asked.

He swayed his head side to side. "Must have started to black out or something. I'm not feeling that great."

I got him onto his feet and we shuffled out into the hall as Mr. Schmoll was erasing that partial list of European wars. "Zeke, Dixon," he addressed us without taking his eyes off his work. "Test on Friday."

I almost told him to fuck off. But that wasn't because he was being rude. It was just the unsettled voice of doom inside me.

We'd heard that Dave was back from Ozzieland and, even though Zeke was feeling less than up to par, he was anxious to share his story with ole FWD. We dropped by Zeke's locker and picked up his skateboard. Then we started walking toward the beach. We were almost there and I saw Dave's familiar van parked in his usual spot. That's when Zeke said, "Dixon, I just feel so tired."

And then he collapsed. It was like he was a puppet and someone had just cut the strings. I thought I heard screaming but I knew it was inside my head.

Dave saw what had just happened and he sprinted from his van. "What's up?" he asked, leaning over Zeke who was out cold.

"We got to get him to a hospital," I said. I wasn't sure he was even breathing. My heart was pounding so fast I couldn't tell.

Dave picked him up and gently put him in the back of his van on the mat on the floor. I hopped in, slammed the door, and we were off, racing through town. I felt the blood rush to my head and heard the screaming louder but did my best to give Zeke CPR. Chest pump, mouth to mouth. I don't know if I did it right or not, but I kept at it and didn't think about the fact that maybe I didn't know what I was doing.

Dave phoned 9-1-1 on his cell and got through to the hospital. For someone who had cultivated such a laid-back, non-affected attitude, he was suddenly all focus and all business.

When we arrived at the hospital, a gurney was waiting with two emergency doctors. They rolled Zeke inside and told us to check in at the desk. Dave and I had been waiting for fifteen minutes when one of them came out. He was looking at a clipboard and never looked up once as he said, "Sudden cardiac arrest. His heart just stopped. It just stopped."

I could feel the darkness all around me then. I couldn't quell the screaming voices in my head. Dave was asking questions and the doctor was trying to answer them the best he could. When I was asked about parents, I gave them Zeke's home phone number and told them to call Brian.

"Can we see him?" I asked.

"You family?"

"No, friends," I mumbled.

"We're only supposed to allow family," the doctor now said, trying to sound apologetic.

"Please?" I asked.

He nodded. We were led into the emergency room. Zeke was lying on his back, eyes closed, peaceful. He had that same expression on his face that he'd had while snoozing in European History. I touched his hand and it was cold.

It all seemed unreal but I knew it was all so very real.

I wondered if he got to experience "everything" one more time.

As Dave drove me home, he just kept saying, "It all seems so fucking unfair."

When he stopped at my house, he asked, "You want me to come in with you and hang out for a while?"

I said, "No, I think I just want to be alone."

"You positively sure?"

"Yeah," I said as I got out of the van. And as I walked to my house, I felt truly alone; I felt more alone than I'd ever felt in my life.

CHAPTER

TWO

What shall I do now? What shall I do?

I won't forget the look in Dave's eyes as he dropped me off at my house. He looked defeated. I don't know why that is the word that fits. But it does. He kept trying to say something soothing to me, something helpful. He was trying to play big brother but he didn't have shit. He was as lost as I was. So all I did was tap once on the dash of his old van. Again, I don't know why. I tapped once with my knuckle and then I got out and prepared to stumble forward into oblivion.

When I walked into my house, I was shocked to see that I was carrying Zeke's skateboard. I must have picked it up inside Dave's van. I almost laughed. I didn't even know I had it. I could hear the TV on. My mom was watching a show about people in New Jersey who made fancy cakes for special occasions. It was one of her favorite shows. I guess I was in shock. I guess I was in denial. It was a foggy, indistinct place and I knew darkness was ahead. I felt that I had somehow known this would happen way back—what, nine days ago. That was what all that journal writing was all about.

I opened up the refrigerator, for God's sake, and I stared at that little light that goes on, remembering my question to my father when I was young.

"Does that light stay on for the food when the door is closed?"

"No," my dad had said.

"How does it know when to go on, then?"

My dad was pretty cool about this stuff and almost never gave a dull, scientific answer. "It hears your footsteps on the kitchen floor, knows when you are hungry, and when you are about to open the door."

"What if I was very quiet and it didn't hear me coming?"

"Oh, it would sense the vibrations on the floor. It would know."

I had tried many times, sneaking up on the refrigerator, and the light was always on when I opened the door. But then one day, I opened the fridge and it was dark inside. The bulb had blown out, I guess, but I had bought into the other mythology. I stared into the dark fridge and felt betrayed. A dark refrigerator had shaken my world. It was that easy.

My father had laughed and took me to a hardware store to buy a new bulb. He allowed me to screw it into place and, when the light came back to the fridge, to the world, I felt that the universe was back to normal. That I was back to normal.

Normal. That's a funny concept.

So there I was: my best friend had died and I'm standing in my kitchen with a skateboard, staring into our family refrigerator, registering the contents: one percent milk, Swiss cheese, leftovers, etc. There on the bottom shelf was a cabbage. It made me think about running away to New Zealand. About being that hermit I had fantasized about.

I know how this all sounds. But, see, I'd never really had anyone close to me die before, so I didn't know the drill. I wasn't angry yet. I wasn't grieving. I didn't know how. I didn't believe that Zeke could be gone. Not just like that. I decided that none of this had really happened at all. I could see that it was me slipping into the dark zone. I was clearly off my ego-super-high. *Boy can save the world, do anything.* That had been some time back. I closed the refrigerator door before the cabbage started speaking to me.

So I called FWD's cell phone. I needed some confirmation that Zeke's death wasn't all in my woeful imagination. He didn't answer and the message just said his mailbox was full. A debate began in my seething brain about what to trust. What information was real? What was just my imagination?

I looked up and around the kitchen and found it was familiar and comforting. But something about it was different. The colors slightly off. The lighting coming in through the window seemed to hurt my eyes. The clock on the wall, the old style with the arms, was ticking and I'd never heard it ticking before.

And then it stopped ticking. And the second hand stopped moving. I held my breath. I had a sudden flash, an image of Zeke in the icy water, splashing. A reminder he had survived that incident. And the dog was okay. And Zeke was okay.

But he wasn't okay. As the clock started ticking again, my mind was sorting out what was real and what was not real and shouting to me that today had been real. One moment you're spinning the wheels on your skateboard with your index finger and thinking about how horny you are for someone's mom. And the next minute, your heart stops and the world for you ceases to exist. Like Dave said, it just isn't fair.

But I slipped back into denial to save my sorry self. I told myself it couldn't have happened that way and tomorrow it would all be different.

I held tight to Zeke's skateboard and went to check on my mom. She was crying. "It's all so sad," she said, pointing to the TV screen and then hitting the pause button on the DVR. "They had such a beautiful wedding cake and then called off the wedding at the last minute."

I felt bad that my mom was crying but knew this was her thing. TV was an outlet for her. She usually got over TV tears fairly quickly, so I thought it was mostly harmless. I knew I couldn't tell her about Zeke. She'd go off the deep end and I couldn't handle that now. "What are they gonna do with the cake now?" I asked.

"They can't resell it. It has names on it. Everybody is so upset. Especially the ones who made the cake."

"It's a bad situation," I said. "Maybe they can donate it to the food bank."

"Maybe," my mom said, resuming the show. Her tears had dried and I headed to my bedroom.

Once inside, I closed the door and sat at my computer. I played a short video Zeke and I had made using Zeke's video camera. In it we had both pretended to be aliens arriving on earth for the first time. Zeke was in a close-up staring at a toothbrush, theorizing on what it was used for. I was holding a leaf up to the sun. We acted goofy and it was a pretty stupid video as we pretended to be aliens agog at the new planet we had found. We jumped around and made weird noises, pretending that was what we did on our home planet. Then, suddenly, Zeke looked at his watch and said to the camera, "Uh, oh. Time's up. We have to leave now." And then the screen went black.

Like I said, it was a pretty lame video, and we meant to post it on the Internet but never did.

I knew there was a door up ahead. Not a real door. But a door, nonetheless. Once I opened that door, things would be different. Once I let Zeke's death sink in, I would go to that dark place. I would face the reality of his death and that would trigger (or as the shrink had once said, "kindle") something terrible in me. I knew I had to go there but not yet. If I kept my denial intact. If I did not get angry. If I just pretended and held it together, I might come up with a plan to save myself down the road when no one else could save me.

I zipped the silly video back to somewhere in the middle. After the toothbrush, after the leaf. The alien Zeke suddenly looks up and around, appearing to be convincingly astounded at the new planet, and the alien me studies him and then says, "What is it you see, commander?"

And Zeke stares straight into the camera, smiles, and says, "Everything. I see everything." I froze that image of him on the screen.

CHAPTER

THREE

I could not
Speak, and my eyes failed, I was neither
Living nor dead, and I knew nothing

Shock. Denial. Anxiety. Fear. And so much more.
So get this. I got up from my computer and walked to my bed and sat down with my head in my hands. When I looked up again, I was completely freaked. Death had arrived to keep me company.

Yes, Death. Death is a person. Death sat down to speak with me. I will say up front that I truly understand what happened. This person in my room was from my imagination. From my condition. But it was as real as anything could be. It was not Zeke coming back from the dead to speak to me. I had hoped and prayed for that. I had actually prayed for Zeke to come visit me one more time. Tie up loose ends. Get a report from the afterlife. Shoot the shit on anything.

But no go.

I didn't recognize him at first—this oh-so-perfect hallucination. He was sitting there at my computer as if he'd just been checking his frigging email. A tall, thin Black man with a short gray beard. He was wearing a blue shirt and jeans and seemed as calm as anything.

It was my school bus driver from when I had been in Grade 7, Mr. Muir. Calvin Muir, who had died in a road accident. Killed in his bus when a kid in a stolen half-ton truck ran a stop sign and smashed into him. Killed just minutes after letting off his last passenger for the day—that would be me.

"Carter Dixon," he said. "Or is it Dixon Carter?" He smiled.

"Jesus," I said. "Mr. Muir."

"Call me Calvin, like back in the day."

I was stunned. Knowing this could not be real, knowing what my mind was capable of, knowing it was some kind of sound hallucination, was not good enough.

"I'm here because of what happened," he said. "I don't usually make house calls. But in your case ... well, you're someone special."

I figured I had no choice but to engage in this hallucinatory conversation. "You're here because of Zeke?"

"I didn't know the lad but he was your friend, right?"

I nodded.

"It hurts when you lose friends. I lost a few in my time. Hey, when my time came, I missed you as well. Remember those conversations we had on the bus?"

"The ones you weren't supposed to get into with kids, right?"

"Yeah, those ones. Shit, we talked about some crazy stuff. You with your Einstein quotes and all that talk about madness. You were one smart but crazy little kid."

"I'm sorry about what happened. I kept thinking that I might have died, too, if that kid in the hopped-up truck had come barreling along a few seconds earlier."

"Guilt," Calvin said. "The living always feel guilty about being alive when someone close to them departs. But I feel honored that you felt that way. Means we had some kind of bond."

"You were about the only one in those days who could talk seriously with me about philosophy or the occult or anarchy."

"Those were your favorite topics of conversation, if I recall." He looked up at the ceiling and then back at me. Remembering one of those conversations, he asked, "If you were a brain in a vat and everything seemed real to you, like you were living normally, would you want to know you were only a brain in a vat or keep thinking that what you were experiencing was real?"

"Yeah, you asked me that one day."

"And you said that you'd want to know the truth."

"I did," I said. "But if you asked me now, I'm not sure. I may want to keep the illusion."

"Illusions have their own intrinsic reality," Calvin said. "Like this one."

"Yeah, like this one," I agreed.

There was an awkward silence. Then Calvin cleared his throat, stood up, and rubbed his chin. "I'm not real sure how I'm supposed to do this. It's a bit like acting. But I seem to be real to me. You know that I'm not a ghost or any of that horseshit. I wish I were, but I know for a fact that you are the one who conjured me up. I'm just not sure what it is I'm supposed to do."

"I'm not sure, either. I'm just trying to deal with this."

"With Zeke, you mean?"

"Of course. See, the funny thing is I'm not feeling bad for Zeke. I'm feeling bad for me. Zeke's off the hook. No more walking to school in a cold rain. No more hassles from teachers. No more worries about grades. No more worrying about what to do when you grow up. Zeke's best guess at what he could do for a living was designing and making custom skateboards."

"The world could have used more of that. But I hear what you're saying. Zeke is in no pain—you are correct. And he has no worries. Once you get rid of your body, you have a whole lot less stress, I can tell you that."

I think maybe he was trying to be funny. "Where is he then?"

Calvin lifted his hands up and looked to the ceiling. "Out there somewhere. Just 'cause you can't see him doesn't mean he isn't there."

I was a bit stumped just then. I had a sudden clarity in one part of my brain. It was like I had taken a step outside of myself and was looking at this boy, this crazy teenage boy talking to the dead school bus driver, talking to his own hallucination. "What is it we are doing here?" I asked suddenly, my voice sounding harsh.

"You know what we're doing here," Calvin said. "Putting off the inevitable. It's a good trick and I'm happy to be here, but soon I'll be gone and you'll have no choice but to deal with the shit that happens next."

"I don't know if I can do that on my own. Zeke was part of my life. He helped keep me sane. We were on the same wavelength. Just the two of us."

"We're talking about your own survival, right?"

"Yeah," I admitted. "I haven't opened that door yet, but when I do, I don't know ..." My voice must have trailed off.

"You don't know if you're gonna be able to make it back."

"I don't know if I will want to come back."

"You're gonna have to talk to somebody."

"That's where you come in."

He laughed a little and then coughed. It was the cough that caught me off guard, made me think he was real. It was a human cough. Then he said, "I'm not always gonna be here. I got a busload of kids I got to drive to school."

I gave him a perplexed look.

"Metaphorically speaking," he added. "We all got a job to do. Zeke did his and he had to move on."

"Don't give me the 'it-was-his-time' bullshit. Not that crap about him dying was meant to be or any of that garbage."

"I wouldn't do that. I have a few thoughts on the big picture, but not necessarily that. I'm just a brain in a vat—

so to speak—and I know I'm a brain in a vat and I'm cool with that."

I was still trying to work this through. If Calvin was not real, then maybe this was all some kind of crazy game going on inside my head. And if Calvin was not real, then maybe Zeke's death was not real. It seemed about as unreal as a thing could be.

"Sorry, Dixie, it's real. And you're gonna have to do what you have to do. I don't see any way around it."

I knew exactly what he meant.

"Problem with you young kids today," he continued, "is you don't believe in God. You have access to too much information; you are overwhelmed with information, but most of it is trivial, and nobody's given you the tools to cope with heavy shit like this."

"Now you're preaching to me."

"Damn straight. Why do you think you brought me here?"

"Then, what am I supposed to do now?"

"Go deep. Real deep. Probably no other way."

He was right. This was all some kind of stall tactic. I could feel the darkness behind me, like some cavern had opened up in my wall and was about to swallow me.

"I see it, too," he said. "You are gonna have to give it some proper names. Madness, despair, depression, darkness, gloom. Whatever you like."

"Don't leave," I said. I really didn't want to be alone. Even a hallucination was better company than being alone right now.

"When the time comes, you'll have to reach out. The

sooner, the better. You gotta do the right thing by Zeke."

"What do you mean 'the right thing?'"

"You got to keep on living. I mean really living."

"That's easy for you to say," I shot back.

Calvin smiled. "Like I said, I got a bus I gotta get back to. Good to see you again, Dixon."

As I sat there, I got my focus back on the computer screen, the frozen image from the video of Zeke, eyes looking straight at the camera, mouthing that word.

And then I felt something cold coming from the gaping cavern behind me. I fought it for a few seconds. I really did. But it was like the gravity of a black hole in space. I tried to focus on Zeke's image but it, too, began to fade. I told myself to hold on, to get up and distract myself.

But I couldn't move.

And then things went black.

CHAPTER

FOUR

Unreal City,
Under the brown fog of a winter dawn

So you wake up on the morning after the day your best friend dies and, at first, you think it was a bad dream. The reality starts to seep in and you fight it. You fight it like hell. You try to go back to sleep, thinking going back to sleep is really waking up. That this morning thing is the dream. But it doesn't work.

I remembered the Calvin Muir conversation and that seemed as real as anything. But then the scene in the hospital came back. And Dave driving me home. And, yeah, it was morning for real and Zeke was gone. Just like in the video. He had departed the planet—only this time, he left me behind. On a planet with sunlight on leaves and toothbrushes. I was an alien on a potentially hostile planet where survival alone, cut off from my own world, would be painful and difficult.

I threw on some clothes, picked up Zeke's skateboard, and went down the stairs and out of the house. My dad's car was gone, so he was at work. And I couldn't sit down with my mom and talk. Maybe they hadn't heard yet, but it wasn't them I needed. I didn't know what I needed. I just started walking.

But then I stopped.

Here was the place Calvin Muir had met his end. I stood on the sidewalk and watched the little puffy clouds of my breath. Maybe I expected Calvin to reappear but he did not. Calvin and Zeke. One minute there, the next minute gone. Does it really work like that? What a shit system. What are the rest of us supposed to do once we are left behind?

I started walking again, thinking that dying is the easy part. Living after a loss like this, that's the hard one. Really hard.

Zeke, you pervert, you stupid piece of shit. Why did you do this to us? Why did you abandon me when I needed you most?

I might have said it out loud. I guess I did. A school bus was going by just then. And kids were staring at me. Madman of the morning. Then the bus rolled on by. It was not Calvin at the wheel—I was sure of that. It was just business as usual. Those little kids inside, innocent brats, off to elementary school and not a care in the world.

The roads were slushy; the air had that winter crystalline

feel to it—cold, clean. No wind. Every breath was a cloud of my own making. Everything appeared so damned normal. If you were in the right frame of mind, you'd even say it was a beautiful morning. Which made me even more angry.

I don't know how long I stood there. There was no one else walking on the sidewalk. Cars drove by, spraying some of the slushy water and snow in my direction, but none of those drivers seemed to care. *Business as usual.* I might have stood like that for a long time. But my cell phone rang. I almost thought it had to be Zeke. I mean, I wanted it to be Zeke, telling me that it was all a mistake. The doctors at the hospital had it wrong, he would say. They goofed. He wasn't dead at all. Still breathing, taking his own sweet time getting to school.

I answered it. "Hey."

"I heard," she said. It was Sylvia. "I don't believe it."

"Yeah," I said.

"Where are you?"

I guess I didn't answer her.

"Dixon? You okay?"

"No," I said. "I'm not okay."

"Is someone there with you?"

"I'm on the street, not far from my house, I guess. No. No one is here. Where are you?"

"School. But I'm coming to be with you."

"Why?" I heard myself say.

"Because this is not a good time to be alone. Don't go anywhere, okay?"

"Okay."

So, I guess I looked pretty strange to anyone who bothered to notice me. After I put my phone away, I looked up into the dead branches of a winter tree. There were birds there, starlings, and they seemed kind of busy, with lots of noise and fluttering around. Something was going on, some bird thing, and I stood there watching them, listening to their raspy little bird noises and seeing them going this way and that, like they were jockeying around for the best places to sit in the tree, like their morning activities, whatever they were doing, were the most important things in the world.

And I did not slip over into the dark place right then, even though I was sure I was headed there. I was again an alien visiting a strange and inexplicable planet Earth. I was still standing like that when a taxi pulled up. Sylvia jumped out and she ran to me.

"Dixon," she said, "you okay?" She was holding my face in her hands. Her face was close to mine and I could feel the warmth of her breath. "I can't believe he's really gone." Then she pulled away and stared at the skateboard I was holding.

"I don't know what to do," I said. "I got this far out of the house, but I can't seem to find any reason to keep going. And if I did, what direction would I go?"

"Tell me what I can do to help."

"Just be with me," I said and she gave me a hug. Sylvia was a true lifesaver.

It was the hug and her presence that got me unstuck. I started to feel the pain, I think, for the first time. The mind-fog lifted and a real, deep-down ache began. But I knew that doing nothing was the worst thing I could do. I suddenly began to think about Zeke's mom and dad.

"Will you go with me to Zeke's house?"

Sylvia looked puzzled. "You sure that's a good thing to do? I mean, are you going to be okay with that?"

"Yeah, I'm sure. I need to do this."

I rang the doorbell about a dozen times but no one answered. Then we both heard a loud noise—something being smashed. I turned the knob and let us in. We heard it again. This time a scream and something smashing. We ran through the house to Brian's studio just as he slammed a sledgehammer into one of his stone sculptures and white chips of alabaster went flying through the room. Brian, a man who had always been quiet and thoughtful and a little odd, was breathing hard as he noticed us. As he turned away, he zeroed in on one more piece, a beautiful large marble egg of some sort. He grunted, drew back the hammer, and then blasted into the egg. Only it didn't break. It rolled from the stand and hit the concrete floor with an unearthly thud.

Brian dropped the hammer to the floor and began to cry. He slouched forward and put his head on a workbench and sobbed. We walked closer.

"Hi, Brian," I said.

Brian sobbed for a minute and then sucked in his breath and looked up at us. His eyes were red and he was still breathing funny. He looked around at the destruction in his studio and seemed embarrassed now. He put his hands up in the air as if he didn't know how it happened.

I nodded. Sylvia squeezed my hand tightly. There was a long silence and then Brian walked over to the big marble egg and sat down on the floor beside it, amidst the rubble of his other destroyed sculptures. "They say his heart just stopped. Happens to one in a million people—and not usually kids. How could it happen to Zeke?"

I was thinking that was the way it would go from now on, maybe forever. Unlimited unanswerable questions. Why this? Why that? Why anything?

I didn't know whether we should just listen or leave or what but I ventured something. "After the dog incident, did he talk to you about being unconscious?"

Brian shook his head no.

"I asked him what he saw and he told me this. He said he saw everything. Everything. And I don't know what that meant. And I never really had a chance to get him to explain it to me."

Brian looked confused at first, puzzled by this tidbit of information about his dead stepson. And then he released a hint of a smile and said, "That is just so Zeke. Just so like him."

I guess I didn't know what else to say. So I walked over to Brian and handed him Zeke's skateboard. Brian took it and held it to his chest.

CHAPTER

FIVE

A heap of broken images, where the sun beats,
And the dead tree gives no shelter

So there I was on some kind of fucking pilgrimage, I guess. I was about to descend into the basement hell of my mental disorder—or whatever they call these things these days. Talking to my dead friend's father—trying to do what, exactly?

And Sylvia trying to keep me alive. Keep me sane.

That familiar dark fog started to creep into me about then. Sylvia could see it and she tried to cover for me. She and Brian kept talking but it sounded to me like it was a foreign language. I watched the conversation as if I was in another room. Brian was squeezing the handle of a hammer that looked like a small version of a sledgehammer. At some point in the conversation, he lifted it high in the air and it looked like he was about to hit her.

But it wasn't that. He let out a scream and swung it, smashing it hard into another one of his stone sculptures that was shaped like a cloud. There was a loud noise and the cloud shattered into more chips of white alabaster that went flying around the room like pieces of shrapnel.

A piece hit me in the chest and I think I felt something, but it wasn't pain. It was like it had happened to someone other than me. A small sharp chip of the rock hit Sylvia on the face and I saw a trickle of blood on her cheek that she quickly covered with her hand. She looked over at me and I knew things were bad.

Brian had turned his back to us. Sylvia took my hand and said something softly to Brian in words that still seemed to be in a foreign language. And then she led me out of there.

Back on the sidewalk, our breath making small puffs of clouds in the air, she asked me, "Are you all right?"

"Yes," I answered from a million miles away.

"Do you want me to walk you home?"

"No," I answered. "I want to go to school."

"You sure?"

"Yes."

At school, everyone knew what had happened to Zeke. People spoke to me but I didn't respond in any way. I convinced myself that I was looking and acting normal but that really wasn't the case. Sylvia kept showing up after each class to walk me down the hall but it didn't feel right.

Nothing felt right. I finally slipped out of math when the bell rang and walked quickly away so she couldn't find me. I don't exactly know why; I just knew I needed to be alone.

That's when Harlem Poodle found me.

Don't laugh. I'd never met anyone like him.

It went like this.

I felt a bit like I'd just escaped from a prison. I wanted to run but didn't know where to run to. Suddenly, there in the hall, this truly bizarre kid was in my face. He had longish greasy hair, thick-rimmed glasses, and a notepad in one hand and a pen in another. "You're Dixon, aren't you? Dixon Carter."

That increased my paranoia and this weirdo could see it for sure.

"Be cool. I'm Zeke's cousin. Let's get the hell out of here. This place gives me the creeps. Then let me explain."

I don't exactly know why I followed him but I did. Zeke had mentioned a couple of his cousins before, told me about one who was a real case. I figured that must be this one. If he was, maybe I needed this connection. I was still lost in the dark caverns of my own sorrow and pity, but I followed.

"Man," he said as we left the building, "how do you put up with all that chaos?" It was snowing lightly outside and the snowflakes seemed to be living things, falling and whirling and each having a mind of its own. This weirdo was buttoning up his coat and looking at his notepad. Lucky for me, I had not taken off my jacket all day. It wasn't a winter coat but something I could get away with in class. Now I felt the winter chill driving through my bones, but it felt good. And I think the snowflakes were singing something, more of a chant than anything with real words.

I followed the guy a few steps out onto the sidewalk and watched as he kept looking at the notepad. I couldn't figure what that was about, so I grabbed it from him and read from the page:

It was a list.

1. Go to the school.

2. Find Dixon Carter.

3. Lead him out of the school.

4. Tell him who you are.

5. Tell him why you are here.

6. Make him understand.

7. Help Dixon Carter.

The kid grabbed the list back and said, "We're only up to number three. Please, keep walking."

I stared at him but I kept walking.

"I'm Zeke's cousin," he repeated. "My name is Harlem Puedel but everyone calls me Harlem Poodle."

It was like some kind of bad sick joke.

"I know what you are thinking. But hang with me. Let me try to explain some things."

"Why do you want to talk to me?"

"Because of 5, 6, and especially 7. Will you go with me to the public library? I like it there. All the books are organized. Everything makes sense."

I guess, at that point, I was happy to be away from school and all those other kids staring at me. I was strangely glad to be away from Sylvia, even though she had been trying to protect me and guide me through the day. All around me, the wasteland was dark and vast and filled with white falling flakes that no longer seemed alive or melodic. It was more like cold white ash falling from the sky. I did not feel the cold seeping in through my thin jacket. All I knew was that I was skipping school and walking toward the public library with a kid with the unlikely name of Harlem Poodle.

In the public library, we found a quiet corner and Harlem began to chatter. It went something like this.

"Let's go at this slowly.

"You'll probably want an explanation for my ridiculous name. So we'll begin there.

"Harriet was my mother and Lemuel was my father. My father's family had an old tradition of combining parts of family names to come up with new ones. So Aunt Margaret and Uncle Gordon begat Margor for the girl and Gormar for the boy. Aunt Linda and Uncle Bradley named their children Linley and Bradda. You can see how this goes and it is both creative in an odd sort of way and a bit ridiculous, which you may see is a theme of my existence.

"Harriet and Lemuel begat Harlem. And, just for the record, I am not Black or Hispanic, have never been to New York City, or have any pretense of being a white rap artist with an attitude. Harlem is just me.

"Poodle is actually a corruption of the French last name Puedell. Pronounced Pyou-dell, but by the time I was in Grade 1, everyone—and I do mean everyone—called me

Harlem Poodle and, like unwanted dog feces jammed into the deep treads of your running shoes, it stuck and it stayed. The association with a white French dog is of no consequence. I like being called Harlem Poodle and so be it.

"When I am introduced to new people, they hear my name and smile. When teachers read out my name on their roster at the beginning of the year, some actually say, 'There must be some mistake, because this says, "Harlem Poodle."' I raise my hand politely and say, 'Yes, that's me.' And of course, kids laugh. But other kids laughing at me does not make me mad or feel embarrassed or humiliated. I am being prepared for great things. Movies, perhaps. I envision *Kings of Destiny* starring Harlem Poodle; or secretary general of the United Nations, Mr. Harlem Poodle; or winner of the Nobel Prize for Physics, Professor Harlem Poodle. I am fairly certain I am destined for greatness.

"But then I think each of us is destined for greatness. Most people just fuck it up somehow along the way and end up watching hockey or wrestling on TV and eating Doritos."

CHAPTER

SIX

Those are pearls that were his eyes. Look!

"Here's the thing," Harlem Poodle finally said. "Zeke knew he was going to die."

"Bullshit," I said, a bit too loud. "That's bullshit and you're an asshole."

"I may be an asshole," Harlem said. "I've been called worse things. But Zeke had this idea in his head. He said he got the idea from a title of a story or something. He said he expected to have a short, happy life."

"What does that mean?"

"Well, just what it means. Short. Happy."

"He should not have died."

"But he did. And he had talked about it." Harlem looked

up at the stack of books around us and swallowed hard. "He knew."

"Knew what?"

"Knew that his days were numbered. He talked to me about it all the time."

"He never said anything about it to me."

"He didn't want to mess with your head. But he talked to me about it because ever since I was a little kid, I expected to die when I was twelve or thirteen. I just knew I was different, would never be like everyone else, and would die young."

"But you didn't."

"No. And it came as a kind of shock. I never planned on being a teenager. I believed I'd come down with an incurable illness and just croak. So I read as many books about the afterlife as I could. I was looking forward to it."

"You are one crazy screwed-up kid."

"Tell me something I don't know. But here's the thing. I prepared myself to die and so did Zeke."

"How did you do that?"

"I lived each day as if that was the one where I might die. You know, croak. Kick the bucket. Bite the biscuit, meet my maker, feed the worms, give up the ghost, buy the farm."

"You think that's funny?"

"Yeah, I do. Laughing at death is the only way to go."

Just then I remembered the look on Zeke's face when he had spoken about nearly drowning in the water. He had been smiling, almost laughing.

"But when I didn't die at twelve, I was sure it would be thirteen. But then I turned fourteen and wondered what was going on. That's when I had to learn to laugh at the joke."

"What joke?"

"The fact that I was going to have to tough it out and become an adult. I'd have to live with being me—different, odd, not really normal, not really part of this world."

"So you are telling me Zeke thought his life was just a big joke?"

"No, Dixon, he thought his death was kind of a joke. He was okay with taking one in the ribs 'cause he lived his life. He really lived it. How many of us can say that?" Harlem looked down at his shoes all of a sudden and saw one of the laces was untied. He bent over, tied it, seemed unsatisfied, untied it, tied it again, undid it, and retied it several times before looking up. "God, I love the library," he said. "Everything is so organized here."

There was that word. "Everything," I said out loud.

Harlem looked more or less satisfied with his latest knot. "What?"

"That's what Zeke said in the ambulance after he had been underwater and drowning."

A slow smile crept over Harlem's face. "Did he really say that?"

I nodded.

"Perfect. That's just perfect." Harlem took out a little notebook and wrote something in it. When he looked up, he asked, "Feeling better?"

I didn't answer because it seemed like an odd shift in the conversation. But, yeah, I felt better. Still confused and hurt, but better. And I didn't know why. "Now what?" I asked, since it seemed like there had been an agenda here and I was along for the ride.

"Now we try to connect the dots. If you are willing to help."

"What dots?"

"Zeke had said something about pulling together those people who would be affected by his death. He said I had to do it. But I need your help. He hinted that if I reached out to you, you'd be a pain in the ass at first and think I was a lepton, but you'd come around."

"What the fuck is a lepton?"

"An insignificant subatomic particle."

"Oh. No, I wasn't thinking that."

"Good. Then you'll help?"

"Help do what?"

Harlem suddenly looked puzzled. He studied his shoelaces again, began to lean over, but then sat back up. "I don't know. We'll have to see."

CHAPTER

SEVEN

I will show you fear in a handful of dust.

Harlem was poking around in his pockets, pulling out little notes. He'd look at each one, and then fold it up and put it back in his pocket. On one scrap of paper he wrote down his email address: melrah_ledeup@hotmail. com, and his phone number. "We're going to need to stay in touch," he said.

"I really don't understand," I said.

"Zeke told me all about you. You're at the center of this thing. I'll help you figure out your role. I'm not sure I know who all the players are, so you'll have to help me. I'll be staying in touch."

He looked at his watch and suddenly seemed real antsy. "Look. I gotta go. Duty calls," he said, sounding nervous and looking fidgety. "I'll send you a text. Keep your phone on from now on."

And he left.

I went home and walked into the kitchen where my parents were waiting for me.

"Dixon," my dad said, "a terrible thing has happened. I can only begin to imagine what this must be like for you. You want to talk about it?"

I shook my head no. I felt like if I opened my mouth, I would scream.

My mom looked like she was about to cry and that made everything worse. "Sit down and talk to us. Please."

I looked at her but had to look away. I just couldn't handle this. I just wanted to get out of there. But I was suddenly hungry, real hungry. So I opened the fridge and saw a plate with aluminum foil over it. I knew my mom had saved the food for me. So I grabbed it, closed the fridge door, and tried to give my parents a look that said I'd be okay. But I couldn't bring myself to speak.

Then I went to my room, ate cold ham, baked potato, and string beans. I saw the darkness around me like a reverse halo. I was wondering if this was the night. The night I would "go away." That's what my parents had said the last time I had an episode. "It was like you went away," my mom had said. "We didn't know if you'd come back."

It's not much fun to talk about depression. Sylvia put up with it. She listened. So did Zeke, but Zeke always tried to put a good spin on it. "You got to be down to be up," he chanted, but the cliché always kind of pissed me off. Now I wished I hadn't been pissed off at him. Funny how different we were. I had my share of mental scars. Zeke, as far as I could tell, only had scars and bruises from skateboard mishaps: foot caught in a rail and head over heels; miscalculated slam into a hickory tree in the dark; full impact into the side of a moving car and the usual concrete stairway grab-some-air-but-land-too-soon sort of injuries. He was proud of all the scars and all the body damage. "Bad moments make for great stories," he would say. "Personal legends."

"Hello, darkness, my old friend." Words from an old folky song that Zeke shared with me once, something his sculptor father had turned him onto.

So I decided to open that freaking little book of poetry by T.S. Eliot that Zeke had given me for my last birthday. I turned to the title poem—"The Waste Land." How appropriate. If I was about to enter my own wasteland, Zeke must have known and wanted to provide some clues as to which direction to go.

I skimmed it from the beginning, this dark, irritating, irrational poem that I'd been reading off and on. Each time I'd gone back to it, I found it to be an intellectual puzzle, but also the ravings of a madman. The only thing that made sense was the title. Everything in the poem itself seemed disconnected.

Fear in a handful of dust.

A heap of broken images.

Your shadow at morning striding behind you.

And then this: *Fear death by water.*

But Zeke had not feared death by water. He trusted the

ice. He trusted everything. As far as I could tell, he had feared nothing. I closed the book.

The darkness could be my friend. I could go away tonight if I wanted. But it had not closed in. I looked off to a forgotten corner of my bedroom. Guess what was there? No, not the ghost of Zeke, not a dream image of Calvin Muir. Instead, I saw dust. Not surprising. When did I ever clean my room? It was what we called dust bunnies when we were kids. Now it seemed more like a small gray cloud or a dim galaxy in deep space, not exactly the dust the poet had spoken of, but dust, nonetheless. There it was if I would accept it: fear in this handful of dust. Okay, so be it. I duly noted that forgotten corner of my room and its dust ball of fear.

And I willed it to stay there, in the far corner, so we could cohabitate. So be it. I took a bite of cold ham.

That's when the text message came through from Harlem: *Nothing is the opposite of everything*, it read. *All the players will need to remember that.*

I nearly threw the damn phone at the wall. Players? This was no fucking game.

Players? I fired back. *Who are the players?*

We are, he replied, *and others.*

I turned my phone off. This Harlem guy was messing with my head. Not exactly what I needed about now. I wanted to be alone with my thoughts, alone in my room. Alone in the fucking universe.

No.

I didn't want to be alone at all.

I wanted darkness.

Emptiness.
I wanted it all to go away.
I wanted me to go away.

CHAPTER

EIGHT

There was a funeral.
I didn't go.

NINE

Do you see nothing? Do you remember
Nothing?

The truth is, I remembered everything. Attendance at Zeke's skateboard accidents, his philosophic meanderings, his casual, easy attitude to accepting life with all its inconsistencies and incongruities. Our endless conversations, our easy friendship.

Easy. Funny word to use since almost nothing in my life seemed to be easy. But with Zeke it was different. We were brothers. Sounds corny. But we were.

My parents understood that I didn't want to go back to school for at least a few days. Maybe more. I was thinking about quitting. Not a brilliant idea, I know, but there it is. Sylvia was texting me a lot, worried. Really worried.

I was having flashbacks of Zeke. Vivid ones. Good times. Good guy. But each image was followed by gloomy thoughts, my brain tilted toward the dark side.

Sitting alone in my room was a bad game plan.

Zeke had been dead for exactly five days. I was on the precipice of a very dark canyon. But I had not taken the step off into the void. I was holding back. Truth is, I don't know what I was waiting for. But I was waiting for something. My mom was out and my dad was working, so I was all alone at home again.

And then the doorbell rang. I looked out. It was Harlem.

He was wearing a long dark coat like the kind that flashers wear. He had on those heavy rimmed glasses and a notepad in hand.

I opened the door and looked at him. I wasn't sure I wanted to invite him in.

"You weren't at the funeral," he said, almost accusatory.

"Funerals are bullshit."

"Not sure you could handle it?"

"Fuck you," I said. I didn't need any crap from this weirdo.

"Zeke explained your condition," he countered, adjusting his glasses. "He told me not to take any of your negative stuff personally. I came prepared for that."

"What's this about?"

"It's kind of a long story, but you'll have to trust me first before I can tell it."

"Trust you? I barely know you."

"But we're linked, whether you like it or not. Zeke was my cousin. But he was also my friend. One of the few people who understood me. Wanna go for a walk?"

Harlem had that nervous thing going on again. He was such a dweeb. I guess I felt sorry for him. "Sure," I said.

I threw on my winter coat, went outside, and closed the door.

"Fifteen," he said.

"What?"

"Fifteen steps from the sidewalk to your door. I'm much more comfortable with twenty."

I shook my head. "Sorry about that," I said sarcastically. "Maybe I can get it fixed."

He nodded, smiled a crooked little smile, and we walked on, breathing in the frosty air. We walked on for a bit in silence. Harlem finally cleared his throat and said, "You'll have to help me with what comes next. A lot of hard work has gone into this, but I'm kind of nervous that I'm the one he put in charge of making this happen."

"Making what happen?" I was getting creeped out by the way he was speaking.

"The resurrection," he said.

"What?"

"Well, that's the term Zeke wanted me to use. But he meant it as a sort of joke. He thought you'd get it."

"It's a bad joke. Don't mess with me. Talk straight." But I knew that it was the kind of thing Zeke would say. He was always speaking about belief in a higher order of something. He just wasn't sure who or what he believed in. Just like me. And he liked to toss religious terms around in unlikely contexts. He spoke of the theology of skateboarding.

Transcendental moments. And hormonal responses with spiritual dimensions.

Harlem looked down at his notepad again. "We're only up to item three. That's you, walking with me. Item three. I wrote it all down. Just like Zeke insisted."

"Jesus, man. Does there always have to be an agenda?"

"Maybe not always. But it helps. I'm just trying to do this right. I've run it through on paper but now it's the real thing."

"The resurrection of Zeke?"

He smiled, "No. Not really. It's more technological than spiritual, but Zeke liked to think the two were connected."

I knew, of course, I was not dealing with anyone who was normal here and I was annoyed by all the mumbo-jumbo. But here I was, and I wasn't about to turn around and go back to my room, "So what is item four?" I asked.

"Sylvia is four. Dave Fairweather is five. Sylvia is the strong one. We need her. Dave is older and can bring perspective. It's all leading up to six."

"Which is?"

"Zeke called it The Gathering. Can you text Sylvia and ask her to meet us?"

"She's in school."

"I know. Tell her to meet us outside. Tell her it's important."

So I did as I was told and almost immediately got a response. *Thank God you finally got in touch*, she replied. *Are you okay?*

Don't know, I answered.

It had begun to snow but there was no wind. We walked on through the sifting heavy flakes until we arrived at the school, where Sylvia was waiting for us. She gave me a hug and I introduced her to Harlem. Harlem seemed uncomfortable, as if he wasn't used to being around girls, but then I was learning that Harlem had a nervous air about him at the best of times.

He walked briskly and we tried to keep up. Sylvia put her arm around me and held on tightly. "I'm glad you didn't go to the funeral," she said. "It was all wrong. The minister kept talking about Zeke, but none of what he had to say sounded anything like Zeke. His mom cried the whole time and Brian looked like he was about to lose it. Once the service was over, I didn't hang around."

"I was there," Harlem said. "I hated it, too. It convinced me more than ever to follow up on what Zeke asked me to do. I did get one good thing from it."

"What?" Sylvia asked.

"This," Harlem said, and handed her a photograph of a dog. *The dog*. "She put it by the casket, but I picked it up when no one was looking. I didn't think Zeke would mind and I wanted to hang onto it for today."

"Gus," I said. "The dog's name is Gus."

"Zeke didn't die because he saved the dog. It might have affected his heart in some way, but he had talked to me all the time about preparing for his own death. I thought it was more like a game, so I played along. We even had a bet as to who would die first. I lost."

It wasn't meant to be funny. Sylvia looked at me,

wondering who this turkey was. I shrugged.

Dave was in his camper van down by the old pier at the beach. He had the door open and I could see him inside hunched over his Coleman stove. He had a beard going now and his hair was uncommonly long. He wore some kind of coat you'd see on a lumberjack. A wet wetsuit was hanging up outside and his board was on top of the van. Dave surfed winter or summer. He especially liked surfing in the snow.

He looked up as we approached the van. I could see he looked tired. He also looked older than the last time I'd seen him. He mustered a smile.

"This is Harlem," I said.

"Welcome, dude."

"Hello," Harlem said stiffly.

"'Sup, ladies and gentlemen?" Dave asked.

"Not sure," I said. "Harlem is ... was Zeke's cuz. He says there's something he needs us all to be a part of."

Dave looked puzzled. "Come in. Let's get down to it."

So we all piled into Fairweather Dave's camper van and he closed the door. Sylvia squeezed my hand tightly. Dave's kettle on the old Coleman stove boiled with a whistle and he turned off the flame.

Harlem took a deep breath and peeked at his little notebook. We all waited. "Okay," he finally said. "A little back history. When I was twelve, I had a vision that I was gonna die soon, so I made a video for Zeke. Only for him. No one else. He was the only one who would get what I had to say. Zeke just went along with it and said, sure he'd watch it if I croaked. But I didn't. And what I had to say kept changing, so I kept doing a new video. In a way, it kept me sane. It was like a diary of my thoughts—my deepest thoughts and beliefs."

"So what does this have to do with Zeke?" I asked. "What does it have to do with us?"

Harlem swallowed hard. "Zeke believed he, too, was going to die when he was young. He said he liked the idea, so I persuaded him to do the same. And he told me who to share it with. You guys. That's why we're here."

"So you're gonna play Zeke's video. Here, now?" I didn't think I was ready for anything like this.

Harlem's hands were shaking as he took out his iPhone.

"Wait," I said. "Have you already seen this?"

"Yeah, I have." He looked pale.

"How do we know it's not some kind of a joke Zeke had going? I don't believe he thought he was really gonna die at all. He kept telling me he was fearless, that he was going to live forever. Maybe he saw it just as a game. It would be just like him to say anything, anything at all, that he thought might be funny. Are you sure he took this seriously?"

"I think it's serious, Dixon. But you knew him as well as I did. What do you want me to do?"

"Go ahead," I said. And then Harlem touched the screen of his phone. His hands were still shaking badly. He set the phone down on the table. The little screen was blank at first. Then, there was Zeke—sitting in his basement on his skateboard, wearing his favorite black T-shirt with the word *Independent* centered on his chest, holding a can of his latest energy drink, Fire.

"Okay," Zeke said. "If you are watching this right now, well, that means ... well, you know what it means." And he paused, took a breath, looked up and away. "So I got a few things I want to tell you."

Dave spoke up now. "Stop. Stop the recording."

Harlem touched the screen of his phone.

We all looked at Dave.

"I can't hear him very well. I got a lot of saltwater in my ears. I wanna hear what Zeke has to say. And I want to get a good look at his face while he's saying it." We waited. "If everybody can chill a little, let's drive. I got an idea."

Dave was almost never insistent about anything, but he seemed dead serious, so we all agreed.

He threw his wetsuit into the back and drove us a couple of blocks to an old warehouse, where we followed him through a metal door and up a long flight of stairs. We went into a large room with random furniture and stacks of books and racks of clothes. It was warm and spacious. Dave asked for the phone and connected it to a big flat-screen TV that had been covered with a sheet.

Sylvia and I sat on a carpet on the floor in front of it. Dave got the TV working and sat down. Harlem stayed standing behind us. A frozen image of Zeke appeared on the screen— larger than life, a hint of something going on in his eyes. But it was Zeke, even though he had the weirdest expression on his face.

Dave held out the remote in front of him and said, "Ladies and gentlemen, the late, great Zeke Smith."

"Okay," Zeke said again. "If you are watching this right now, well, that means ... well ... you know what it means. So I got a few things I want to tell you."

CHAPTER

TEN

He passed the stages of his age and youth
Entering the whirlpool.

On the big screen, Zeke paused, took a deep breath and seemed to be looking around the room he was in. Dave got up and walked across the floor to a refrigerator, opened it, and cracked open a beer. I realized this warehouse pad was his back-up when he got tired of living in his van.

My eyes went back to the screen. Zeke had some kind of half-smile going, one I'd seen a million times before, usually when he was saying something outrageous, which more often than not turned out to be not just a goof but something he really meant. He rolled back and forth a little on his skateboard. And then Zeke continued.

"I had the feeling from the time I was a little kid that I

wasn't really meant to be here in this time and place. It wasn't a bad thing, just a sense that I was different. And I expected to die young. That, too, was not so bad. Meant that I had to live every day as if it really mattered. I had to extract every morsel of living life from everything. Not just fun. Though fun was part of it. I had to find joy in stuff. And I know that I was pretty down to earth, so to speak, when it came to looking for the fun stuff.

"School got in the way of real life sometimes. But it gave me down-time to ponder. Friends meant a lot to me. And now that I'm gone—and, sorry dudes, I don't know how I died, but you do—now that I'm gone, I need to say my farewells.

"But that's the coolest part. It's not really *adios*, goodbye, *sayonara, arrividerci*. It's something entirely different."

He looked away from the camera again and he chuckled. Yes, chuckled. I was wondering if he was a bit high on his Chowder House weed. Could be, knowing Zeke.

"No, no, no, I'm not trying to give you the impression I'm going to be suddenly appearing out of thin air in Ms. Bartley's English class next week. That would be a blast, though. Bang. Me, suddenly appearing in the front of the room, naked probably, out of thin air. What would Ms. Bartley do with me? Send me to the office? What would my sudden reappearance do to that ole school? How would modern education techniques cope with such a phenomenon?"

He was giggling now. And, yes, it was apparent, he must have been into the weed. He took a sip of Fire and tilted his head back. Whatever was going on here, Zeke had enjoyed the recording of his post-burial commentary.

"But seriously, folks. These words from the afterlife, so to speak, are sponsored by ..." (he looked around the room again, eyes upward) "... well, by no one. Nothing. And of course, everything."

There was that word.

"Funny thing is, what I have to say to you, my cherished friends, is nothing new. It's good old news that's been around for centuries. But you need to hear it and you need to hear it from me. Here's why.

"People used to believe in God, but something happened and they tuned out. Not because God (or some big kahuna spiritual something) doesn't exist anymore. Just that people mucked it up so badly. The R word. I can't bring myself to say it. It doesn't work well for most of us anymore, so we resort to booze and drugs or surfing or skateboarding. It's all pretty much the same—which I know sounds criminal. But it's all connected.

"We're all connected. We just don't see it.

"We know it deep down and it scares the shit out of us, so we mask it. We wear different clothes, listen to different music, create strong opinions about each other. And we think it's all about the great manufactured god of Me with a capital M.

"But fuck me, what's that about? So I am coming to you from the afterlife—or what I believe will be an afterlife—without a strong sense of what I might actually be at the point you are watching this. My gut feeling is that wherever I am, whatever form of being or spirit or energy that I've been transformed into ... well, I know that it is just fucking amazing."

Sylvia had leaned into me now and I put my arm around her. I wasn't sure if she was really scared or moved in some powerful way. Still, her eyes did not leave the screen. I looked around quickly and noted Dave was holding his beer bottle halfway to his mouth like a scene in a movie where you hit pause and it freezes.

Harlem had his hands clasped together and was intently looking at the image of Zeke.

"So you're all a little sad about me leaving the party. Okay, okay, probably more than sad, if that doesn't sound too egotistical. Teenager dies unexpectedly, old dude at the funeral says stupid stuff about him that has next to nothing to do with the real kid. People cry, undertakers do whatever the hell undertakers do, and next thing you know, life goes on.

"Now comes the hard part. The hard part is me, here today—whatever today is—with a request. Asking you to live your life differently. Sure. Sure. I know, life can be hard. Who am I to ask you to do more than just survive, hang in with the bare minimum, and just let life have its way with you? But I *am* asking.

"As you recall, I was no great striver. B minus was fine for me. But that was school. In other arenas of life, I always wanted to go the distance. Didn't always succeed. Got lots of bruises and bumps for it. But that was my religion, my spiritual quest, although it probably didn't seem so spiritual to anyone but me. Well, and maybe Dixon."

He lowered his head and laughed again. "Shit, now I said the R word. The gospel according to Zeke. Wasn't there an Ezekiel in the Bible? Of course there was. I read that chapter once, only 'cause of the name. Ezekiel was a prophet. Some crazy shit in there but some cool stuff, too. All religions have some good stories to tell. But I'm probably rambling.

"Time to address a few things, campers." He turned his head and looked off to the right. "Yo, Sylvia, you out there?" But he wasn't looking at Sylvia and, of course Sylvia had not been in the room when this was recorded. "Sylvia, we never spoke that much but I always liked you. You were like Einstein Girl, I know, and that was a bit of a burden. Smarter than your teachers, ahead of your time, able to exceed what was expected. But always held back. Maybe you need to just forge ahead and leave the rest behind. Go deep. Not just academic shit. Get outside of that box and go for it.

"But don't give up on my good bud, DC. You've been good for him. He loves you. He told me that. Mr. Deep and Dark and ready to bury himself in a cave. I'll get to him in a minute but, for now, listen up. New Zealand is not for you. Not now. Maybe when you both turn sixty, Dixon will be bald and paunchy but still kicking. You will have a Nobel Prize in neuroscience. Then go raise cabbages. Your kids will be grown up by then as well."

He paused again. Sylvia had pulled away from me slightly and had a puzzled look on her face. Dixon turned to his left. "And brother Dave, Surfer Dave, fellow traveler."

Dave took that sip of beer, a big slug which made his Adam's apple move up and down.

"Sir David, I appreciated the asylum you provided for the likes of Dixon and me. Things in the so-called real world would get a little chaotic and we'd come to chat with you in your kingdom by the sea. You were our guru. You had already cast off the usual rules and regs, and you had written your own handbook for living. You are a good soul and the surf has been kind to you and you have been kind to the surf. But I believe you are ready for the next phase.

Dave spoke out loud now. "Which is?"

Zeke laughed as if he had actually heard him. "Which is … dropping back in. You kicked out, man. You bailed. And it was the right thing to do. But the next wave is coming. It's steep and fast and overhead—the way you like it—and it's all yours. So go for it."

Enigmatic? Yes, but appropriate in a *weird* way. Zeke with his overblown surf imagery. Dave's jaw dropped slightly but there was a hint of a smile. He seemed to know what z-man was talking about.

Zeke's eyes turned again. "Harlem P. This is an odd one, 'cause you actually are here. Thanks for filming this, duder. Just keep to code and don't share until the time comes."

Harlem hit pause. Zeke froze. "Why don't we skip this, guys? Yes, I was there filming. Zeke talked about doing this, but I didn't think he would go through with it unless I was there. He wasn't good with technology and he kept getting distracted, so I told him, one rainy afternoon, to cut the crap and say what he needed to say. It was my job to keep this intact."

"We'd like to hear it," Sylvia said. "It's Zeke, after all. We want to hear all of what he has to say."

Harlem rubbed his hands together and shook his head no. Then he stared at the image on the screen again and seemed to change his mind. "I guess it's okay," he said. He hit the remote and Zeke picked up where he left off.

"Har, you and I go way back and I know how hard things have been for you. What was easy for me always seemed to be a struggle for you. But I think, in the end, that may make you stronger. You are not going to be the one to die young and so you are going to have a hell of a lot more challenges, bro. Don't carry that old sticky label around in your head. You gotta hold your head high and wave that difference you have like a flag, buddy. Be the Republic of Harlem. You live alongside the world but not in it. Like I said to Dave, you may have to dive back into the deep end of the pool and see if you can swim. I see you as a survivor. I trust you deeply. You're the caretaker of this film project. When you get an Oscar for it, be sure I at least get a little credit. You took charge and made this happen. Maybe I got it all wrong and we'll watch this together when we're fifty years old. Or maybe not. Maybe the others need to see this, and they will, because of you. And I thank you for that.

"So be strong. Don't hide your head in the sand. Find a girl, too. She's out there. Put it on the list."

Zeke looked a little tired, like he was running out of steam. I wondered if he was ready to give up on this little game. He took a sip of Fire, rolled back and forth on his skateboard a little, and sucked in his breath. I know he was just guessing, just trying to be theatrical, but he succeeded in turning his head again and looking right at me. "Last but not least, here's some thoughts for you, Dixon. You heard what I had to say about Sylvia. And all four of you have this bond. One dead Zeke linking four living friends.

"You've been planning your escape for too long, my friend. We all have our deep and dark canyons to walk down into. But we all want it to be a short hike and an easy climb up. You've been planning your expedition for a long while. You want it to be deeper and darker than everyone else's.

"And you don't want to come back."

He stared straight at me. There was an ominous silence.

"Whatever shit has hit the fan here, I think you'll want to use it. As an excuse. But I can't let you do that. And you can't let it happen. And Sylvia will be there for you, and Harlem and Dave, but you'll still want to go there. And that sucks, man. You can get yourself so fucking lost that you won't be able to do anything but wallow in it. Yeah, maybe wallow in it so long and hard that, well, it could kill you. I was teasing you with that 'Waste Land' thing. It was so you. I thought maybe it gave voice to the dark and the chaos and the hopelessness. But it is not where you should end up. It's a guide to steer you clear of all that shit. You need to find the road—'The road winding above, among the mountains.'

"I'm thinking that maybe if you eliminate the lows, you may never feel the highs that you once had. Man, I envied you. You'd get so buzzed without doing any drug. I didn't know how you did it until I saw you on those bad days.

Phew, must've taken courage to weather through it. So use that courage. Build on it. That's what Zeke says. Gospel of Zeke, remember?

"That's almost it. Only one more thing. Now, you may be rolling on the floor laughing at this point, I don't know. I'm just speaking what I feel. This is all real to me. I'm still alive but, yeah, I have this gut feeling. Could be soon. Or later. Or way down the long winding road.

"And hey, you've been patient with me. Or not. Maybe you've all gone out for sushi, I don't know. So have some fun in my honor, my memory. And here's the promise.

"You will see me again."

Zeke looked up and away. He smiled that big shit-eating grin and then couldn't help but laugh again. And then the screen went black.

CHAPTER

ELEVEN

The awful daring of a moment's surrender
Which an age of prudence can never retract

The screen remained black as Dave switched off the
TV. He looked at each of us, then shook his head and
went to the refrigerator and took out a beer. "Anybody want
anything?" he asked.

No one said a word. "We're good," Sylvia said finally to
cut through the awkward silence.

Dave cleared his throat. "I've been around longer than
you guys. I've seen some weird shit in my day. But nothing
quite like this. Gonna take me a while to process, you know?
I mean, I should have some brave words for you all right
now but I don't." Dave was a little rattled, but then I guess I
was, too, and so was Sylvia. But not Harlem.

I looked at him. "You were there when this was filmed, right?" I asked.

"I was the one filming the video," he answered. "And Zeke filmed me right after. I did one, too. Only I'm still here. He isn't. We had a pact that whoever went first ... well, the other one had the job of finding the right people and screening it for them."

For some reason, I was feeling antsy again. Agitated. I was angry, too, and I didn't exactly know why. "This is all just bullshit, right? Zeke liked his games. He liked to mess with people. He was just fooling around, right?"

Harlem shook his head and scratched at a spot on his left hand. "I don't know. I mean, I took my version seriously."

"You gonna show us that, too?"

"No, I erased it. It spooked me. The thought of me giving a speech after I was gone. Besides, I didn't really have anyone to share it with."

"I think this is a kind of sick joke," I said, the anger still welling up. I felt like whacking Harlem.

Sylvia squeezed my hand again. "We don't know if it's a joke. Let's not write it off."

Dave took another slug of beer and nodded. "Agreed. Let's give it some time to settle in."

Harlem, Sylvia, and I left Dave's warehouse crash pad in a state of confusion and began walking. It was late afternoon and the winter sun was dipping down behind the buildings. Harlem said he was going to go home, and that was a good thing because I was feeling pissed at him. I still wasn't sure why but I would figure it out soon enough.

I walked Sylvia to her house. "You wanna come in for a while?" she asked. "I'm sure my folks will leave us alone and give us some space."

"No," I said. "I need some time on my own."

"I'll call you," she said and gave me a hug. As she did, I became aware that Sylvia's hug was now the hug of a friend, not a girlfriend. Not a lover. Something had changed. It began to dawn on me how true this was. We had a bond, for sure. But somehow everything was different now. Everything.

At home, my mom was watching TV but my dad was sitting at the kitchen table, working at his laptop. I sat down across from him and he gave me a soft, sad look, then took a plate full of leftovers out of the fridge, placed it in the microwave, and turned it on.

"I called Dr. Stevens today," my dad said. "You know, just to see what he thought we should do. You don't mind that I did that?"

"I guess not," I said. They were both worried about me. "And?"

"And he advised you go back on the meds. Maybe just for a month. This is all pretty hard on you, Dixon. We know you've had a big loss. This could go badly." My dad was a good guy. He'd done a lot of reading about my condition. He'd always tried to do the right thing for me. But I had always wanted to do everything my way. Now, though, I was thinking maybe he was right.

"Let me think about it for a few days," I said. I had a lot I wanted to think about.

My dad looked really worried, but he nodded okay.

The little bell rang on the microwave and Dad took the plate out. It was leftover turkey, with mashed potatoes, turnips, Brussels sprouts, and stuffing. The food was steaming and the plate was hot. Dad almost dropped it as he waltzed it to me, holding onto it with the sleeve of his shirt over his hand.

Food had been the farthest thing from my mind, but suddenly I was hungry. My father sat back down at his laptop and pretended to be working. But he was watching me eat, saw that I had a good appetite. He looked up at me, smiled, and shook his head.

Afterwards, I went up to my room and threw myself on my bed. My mind was in turmoil and I felt a thousand unresolved feelings. I was still pissed off at Harlem and at Zeke. But it didn't really make sense. Why was I angry?

I was tired of thinking about Zeke, about the video. I flicked on my computer to watch something to distract me. I called up *Dogtown and Z-Boys,* one of Zeke's all-time classic films about legendary skateboard pioneers from the 1970s. It was raw and edgy, and every time someone wiped out, I remembered what Zeke had said: "I like the wipeouts best. When I fall off, when I feel the pain, when I try something scary, and fail. Don't know why but it reminds me that all I have to do is keep trying, keep pushing my limits, and, sooner or later, I'll break through. The pain makes it real.

The possibilities make it interesting." I may not have the words just right but that was the idea.

The wind was howling now outside my window and, for some reason, it was comforting. I paused the video and looked out into the dark night. There was a full moon. I'd felt it before I saw it. Yeah, like many other wackos out there in the world, the full moon did tug at something. It made us restless, kept us from sleeping, made us crazier. As I stared at the full silver face of the man in the moon, I saw an image from my memory of Zeke, skateboarding in winter and barreling down a steep sidewalk and out onto the pure glassy surface of Zimmer's Pond, slipping his board on the smooth surface one way and then another in a crazy wonderful dance. In the end, he slid right across the pond and into an old willow tree. He hit hard and fell to the frozen ground but stood up smiling.

Suddenly I was no longer mad at Harlem for what he had shared.

And I wasn't mad at Zeke. Somewhere in my head, he was still zooming across that frozen surface, hell-bent, ignoring good sense, and defying gravity itself. And the ice was solid. It was not cracking. He was in a kind of free flight. And maybe I'd been jealous that he was willing to risk everything and not hold back. While I was almost always holding back. Worrying. Wondering with dread when I would dip into darkness.

I threw myself back down on my bed and stared up at the ceiling.

And there, alone in my room, the wind whistling in the

winter trees, I began to realize something. I was not going to go into that deep dark pit.

The realization was both energizing and frightening.

Zeke had cut off my escape route. Up until today, up until the video he left us, I had felt the pain, the loss. And I knew I had a right to feel that way. And I knew that soon I could let myself slip into the abyss and not care if I ever came back. But something had changed in me. To allow myself to go there would be a total cheat. A cop-out. A complete failure of nerve and will.

And if I went down that dark path, I would be dishonoring the memory of Zeke. And I'd only be punishing anyone who ever cared about me.

I took a deep breath and suddenly felt a new exhilaration. Was it the full moon? The old familiar manic mood swing?

No, it was something different, this feeling. Some kind of awakening, I think. I had this inner vision of me as Zeke— flying across that ice on his skateboard, dancing his board across that frozen pond. And it felt great.

Until I hit the willow tree. And felt the pain.

But there was no darkness.

Only me, lying on my back, looking up at the ceiling, feeling the loss, feeling the uncertainty of every future day of my life.

But I knew now that I was not going to surrender.

CHAPTER

TWELVE

I sat upon the shore
Fishing, with the arid plain behind me.
Shall I at least set my lands in order?

I guess it shouldn't have surprised me that I would have at least one more message from Zeke. It came as an email message two nights later at exactly midnight. It came by way of Harlem, of course. I was alone in my room when it arrived. I had already decided to go back to school the next day and return to some kind of normal activities, even though the thought of school filled me with dread.

Harlem began:

I didn't know if I should send this along to you. Zeke
entrusted it to me but I'm pretty sure he was high when he

wrote it. I don't know why he wrote it or why it is supposed to go to you. It almost sounds like something he wrote for an English class. But maybe it will mean something to you.

And by the way, if we could still be friends, I'd like that. I need all the friends I can muster. I really miss Zeke. Over and out.

Harlem Puedel

And then there was the forwarded message from Zeke, dated just three days before the dog incident and four days before his death.

Hey DC,

I've been trying to piece it all together, trying to make everything make sense. Just like you, dude, I came across a story and it's somehow connected to that T.S. Eliot poetry book I gave you with the poem that totally blew my mind, even though I didn't know what it meant. Yeah, "The Waste Land." You never told me if you liked it or if it made any sense to you. What's with that, dude?

Anyway, the story I came across goes like this.

Once upon a time (can you believe that?) there was a king who lived during the time of King Arthur. He was in charge of taking care of the Holy Grail, which was the cup that Jesus Christ drank out of at the Last Supper. (Are you with me so far?)

Now, this should have been a most excellent thing because the cup was sacred and could be used to perform miracles that the king could have done for his people. But this particular king is not real focused on his job. Instead, he likes to fight, and he gets into some kind of battle where he ends up getting wounded in the balls. And now he can't walk and he can't have sex or have his own kids. He becomes known as the Fisher King because all he wants to do is sit by the river and fish.

As a result, everything in his kingdom goes to crap. Crops fail. It doesn't rain and the country is turning into a desert. People are poor and starving and the soil is dead and dry. I don't know why this would happen, but it does—and keep in mind, this was a long, long time ago and maybe life had a different set of rules.

Different knights come to visit the Fisher King and try to get him off his ass and back into doing kingly duties to get his kingdom back in shape. But they all fail.

But then along comes this younger knight named Percival (great name for an old-time dude!) who had been raised by his mother in a forest so he wouldn't be corrupted by the ways of the world. Somehow, Percival heals the Fisher King. Maybe it was some special herbal medicine he brought from the forest. (Could have been some herbs they smoked, maybe.) And lo and behold, the Fisher King is healed and the barren lands of his kingdom are no longer barren. It rains and plants reappear and people can grow crops again. And the king goes back to using the Holy Grail for good deeds.

End of story. At least that's all I got. I'm not sure I understand the point of the story. But it made me think about you and me, bro. The funny thing is, though, I don't know which one of us is Percival and which one is the Fisher King.

But I'll leave that for you to decide.

Oh, and one more thing, brother Dixon: that little poetry book I gave you, I do want you to get rid of it. It won't do you any more good. I meant it as a sort of travel guide but you won't be going there anymore so you won't need it.

Cheers and good tidings,

Zeke

CHAPTER

THIRTEEN

These fragments I have shored against my ruins

My mom and dad were both thrilled to see me arrive at breakfast the next day at 7:30. My mom made me French toast and both parents noted I still had a good appetite. They were cautious and didn't say too much. I ate, grabbed my book bag, and sent a text to Sylvia that I would head her way and walk her to school.

The sky was clear and the snow was melting, and there was a hint of warmth in the air. It had been a hard winter and it was starting to break.

"You gonna be okay?" she asked.

"Yeah," I said. "I think I am. Zeke's still coaching me. I never fully understood how complex he was. I think he had created this kind of mask that made people think he was just another slacker."

"Maybe it gave him the freedom he needed to live the way he wanted to."

"He lived large. And he was one hell of a teacher."

Sylvia nodded.

Lance was hanging out in front of the school when we arrived. He was leering at Sylvia and then he shot me a dirty look. I was already starting to feel the anxiety and dread settling in. I'd been fighting it. But seeing Lance, sensing his meanness, made me want to lose it.

"Just walk on by," Sylvia said. She could feel my tension.

There was a part of me that still wanted to feel physical pain. I had been tempted to do something in previous days. Cut myself maybe. Maybe something worse. I had fought it off and fought well. I was on the upside of things, but knew I was still walking along that precipice with a big drop below. One step the wrong way and that would be it. But here was a golden opportunity to feel pain.

I stopped and stood directly in front of Lance. He looked at me with hate in his eyes. I could feel his breath. I was standing that close. I could smell him.

"What do you want, freak?" he snarled.

I knew I could say any number of things and he'd lose it. I was ready to taste my own blood.

But then a sudden calmness came over me. It was like a cool clear pool of liquid deep inside me. And it seemed to flow out from somewhere at the center of me, filling every part of my body.

I guess Lance sensed it from the look on my face. His hate

slowly changed to confusion. Suddenly, I realized I was smiling. It was a soft, sad smile because now I was feeling sorry for Lance. But it was more than that. I was feeling compassion for him, if that is the right word.

Sylvia was tugging at me and that deep-seated feeling of calm gave way to something else. My legs felt wobbly. Lance still just stood there. I heard one of his buddies say something like, "What the fuck?" But I was being tugged away by Sylvia and now looking around at the faces of other students who were staring at us. Some, I suppose, had been hoping for a fight. But many just looked worried.

"What was that all about?" Sylvia asked.

"I don't know," I said. "Sorry." I swallowed hard.

"You sure you can handle this?"

"I guess I'll find out," I said.

We were inside the building and Sylvia walked me to my English class. She gave me a kiss on the cheek and smiled. I smiled back.

Ms. Bartley read an excerpt from Ernest Hemingway's novel, *The Sun Also Rises*, a passage about ... of all things ... fishing.

I almost laughed out loud. But I didn't. I knew I'd have to read that book. I had a feeling there was a message in there for me. I was starting to see a pattern to things. Connections. It felt like a fog lifting and a bright light shining through. And it wasn't just moonlight this time. It was the light of the sun.

But I cautioned myself. I'd been there before, too. The sudden, ecstatic, natural high. It had been part of my condition ever since I turned twelve.

The rush, the buzz, the *aha*, the tapping into some grand life energy. Almost anything could trigger it. It was what the meds killed. The high highs that were sacrificed to keep away the low lows.

And the higher the high, the lower the lows.

So I brought myself back down. I was still sitting in English class. I had not moved. Ms. Bartley was asking Rebecca Roberts what she thought Hemingway had meant. Rebecca was a shy girl. Not so pretty. Not so confident. She was having a hard time coming up with an answer and I felt her anxiety, her fear of embarrassment. I felt her pain.

I guess that's why I cleared my throat and blurted out an answer myself. "I think that what Hemingway is talking about is the fact that we are all connected. None of us is alone. We are all in it together. Your pain is my pain. My joy is your joy." I guess I was just giving voice to the thoughts going through my head.

Ms. Bartley blinked and looked oddly at me. My answer, of course, had nothing at all to do with the passage she had read, the one about fishing in a river.

I found myself smiling.

"Very interesting, Mr. Carter. Very interesting, indeed," she said, letting me and Rebecca off the hook completely. "Anyone else care to take a stab at the answer?"

I suppose I drifted after that, just drifted off, as I'd done a million times before. But I'd realized then what I had felt, staring at Lance, and what I'd felt about the crowd outside the school. I'd spent a lifetime of worrying about me, about trying to hold it together. Of either wanting to rule the world or give in to it and let it steamroll over me as I fell into my deep, dark pit.

But now I knew it wasn't about me at all.

CHAPTER

FOURTEEN

Who is the third who walks always beside you?

Zeke, naturally, was right. My days in the wasteland were over.

On Saturday I walked with Sylvia down to the river. We stood there on the bank, the place where Zeke and I had watched the dog trying to drag itself up on the breaking ice. The sun was bright. There was no wind. The water was moving now, although it still had thousands of small islands of ice, each of them a different shape, all of them gleaming in the sunlight like diamonds. Some were small pans of flat ice, others jagged peaks of miniature icebergs.

"It's so beautiful," Sylvia said.

I told her about the latest message from Zeke. She listened and then looked off at the field of moving ice, shielding her eyes from the bright sun.

"Do you think there's more?"

"I don't know. I could ask Harlem, but I don't think I will. Harlem's like the keeper of the secrets, the sacred texts of Ezekiel."

"Was that his real name?"

"Yeah. It was. I didn't know that until I read the obituary. He would have hated being written up with his full name, Ezekiel Emmanuel Smith. What a label. The one and only."

"I miss him."

"Me, too. But he gave us some kind of path. He left instructions." I almost laughed when I said it. "Who the hell gives instructions to his friends when he dies? What kid does that?"

"We're going to get past this, right?"

By "we" she mostly meant me. "Oh, yeah. But first I gotta deal with this." I held up the little poetry book. "Zeke said to get rid of it."

I had thought about throwing it in the river but, on second thought, I reckoned Zeke would appreciate something a tad more dramatic. So I had brought matches—the good old-fashioned strike-anywhere wood matches. I found a dead branch by the river and poked it around in the moving water, until I could pole in a small flat island of ice the size of a large frying pan. I made a tent of the little book right in the middle of the ice and I tried to light it. It took three tries but finally I had a flame.

When I was sure it wouldn't go out, I pushed the little ice island out into the moving water. The flame licked at the sky as the book burned.

"A good old-fashioned book burning," I said. It was meant to be ironic. Usually books were burned for all the wrong reasons, but not this time. We both watched as the book continued to burn. After a few minutes, all we could see was a small tendril of smoke drifting up into the clear blue sky.

"*Shantih shantih shantih*," I said out loud. The last three words of the poem. Peace peace peace.

As the smoke faded in the distance, I think Sylvia understood that we were saying goodbye to a lot of things. I don't exactly know why, but I was feeling good. Not sad, but good. And began to believe that there were good days ahead. We'd move on without Zeke. Or with him, depending how you wanted to look at it. Zeke had prepared the way. Even though I had no idea *what* the way was.

As we walked off, not speaking at all, I felt a familiar wave of euphoria sweeping over me. I had energy. I had ideas. I had a feeling I could take all this and turn it into something magnificent. I started walking more and more quickly, and talking faster and faster. Sylvia looked at me strangely.

"Slow down," she said. She was worried.

I realized I was sweating and breathing rapidly. I couldn't look at her and hold her gaze. My eyes were darting around. "There's so much," I began. "So much that needs to be done. So much for me to do. But I can see it clearly now. I know what I can do to make a difference."

But I didn't know, really. I just had that old gut feeling that I could do anything I set my mind to. I was feeling that old familiar high. My thoughts were racing.

"Slow down," Sylvia said again.

I was turning around and around, as if I needed to see everything around us in the full 360 degrees at once. As if I wanted to see it all, to breathe it all in, to fully appreciate the greatness of the moment and the beauty of the world.

I was still spinning when Sylvia grabbed me hard on the arm. "Stop."

And I stopped. I stopped revolving and let the world settle back down. I waited for my mind to stop racing, my eyesight to gain focus. I was looking straight at Sylvia. I was thinking how beautiful she was. And I think I knew she would not always be with me on my journey.

We walked for at least two hours after that as I began to settle down. We didn't talk about Zeke. We talked about school. We talked about growing up. We talked about some of the old stuff that had been part of our conversations—Einstein, Princeton, New Zealand. And I felt myself coming down. My legs were getting tired and it was getting cooler again by the time we shuffled into the familiar coffee shop and had hot cocoa together. I knew what she was trying to tell me without her having to say it.

The manic high would always be followed by the dismal low. And I had burned my guidebook. I would not need to navigate my way around the wasteland I feared so much. I was not allowed to go there anymore, anyway. I simply wasn't. Who made that rule? Zeke?

No, I did.

Once I got back home, I told my mom and dad that I wanted to make an appointment with Dr. Stevens. I wanted to go back on the meds. But I wanted the lowest dose possible. And I wanted the one that I could stop somewhere not too far down the road. The one I could eventually say goodbye to when I wouldn't need it any longer. We had a long discussion and I felt closer than ever to both of them. I thought my mom was going to cry. But she didn't.

And my dad was like a rock. "We'll be behind you every step of the way."

Two days later a package arrived in the mail. There was no return address and it was neatly wrapped in brown paper, taped meticulously on every edge so it was hard to open, even with a box cutter.

When I finally got it open, I saw that it was a book. The book had a strange vibrant cover with lush foliage and was titled *The Promised Land*. As I flipped it open to the first page, there was an inscription:

On to the next adventure, it said. *Best regards, Zeke.*

And the rest of the book was empty, nothing but pure empty white pages throughout.

And when I closed the book and flipped it over, there was no text at all on the back cover, just a small author photo. A head and shoulders shot of me that Zeke had taken with his cell phone on a warm day in June.

CHAPTER

FIFTEEN

The meds got me through high school. The meds and Sylvia. And nighttime study sessions at the public library with Harlem, who came up with a systematic coaching system to get me through chemistry and math, my two most difficult subjects. And Dave. Dave was there for me, too.

I missed the high days but not the lows. I knew I wasn't going to stay on this drug forever, but it was working. I still got depressed sometimes, but not in any monumental way. I was close enough to being normal to keep functioning, yet I hadn't really found what I was looking for.

I'd written some stuff—mostly rambling—in the empty book, but I sure as hell hadn't found the Promised Land. I couldn't see it on any horizon and I sure didn't have a road map. I think that, for a while, I kept expecting Zeke to magically appear in some form or another. One of those phantom from-the-past emails or a video planted on YouTube or something. But Harlem said he had nothing more for me. Aside from the library coaching from him, I was on my own.

Zeke's stepdad started crying when I showed up at his door one day. He gave me a beer and we talked. Well, *he* talked. Stories about Zeke. Then he pointed to a stone he was carving. "It's like a monument, I guess, to Zeke," Brian said. "I don't even know what it is. But it was a picture that was planted in my head—half-bird, half-fish. I'm gonna put it in the backyard."

"Nice," I said, sipping the beer, wondering if it might interact with my meds that clearly warned not to drink alcohol with the drug. I didn't get the sculpture at first, but then what did I know about art? And then I asked him if I could have Zeke's old skateboard.

"My dad said I needed to be doing something physical, something to get the dopamine moving in my brain, or something like that. So I thought if I had Zeke's old board, well, maybe I could get into it."

Brian walked right over to a closet and lifted it out. He handed it to me and I rolled the wheels the way I remembered Zeke doing. I felt a chill run down my spine at the sound.

But I wasn't much of a skateboarder. I'd go down near the beach and jump some stairs, grind on some railings, and cruise sidewalks and streets. But I got slammed too many times. Concrete was hard and metal was not forgiving, and the hood of a car was relatively soft for a landing, but when you bounced and hit the street, there was pain involved. I had two trips to Emergency but no broken bones.

It was Dave who scraped my sorry ass off the street one hot summer day. "Dude, this ain't gonna work," he said. "Come with me."

I followed him to the warehouse where we had once watched the ghost of my best friend speak to us. It had been dramatically converted into a true luxury pad. He lifted a shiny new surfboard off the wall—a longboard, a nine-foot nose rider, to be precise. "I designed this special. I was waiting for the right kid to give it to. When I saw you splayed out on the street by that Kia, I knew it was you. I call this board 'Salvation.'"

And he laughed.

"Next up, we're gonna teach you to surf. You'll suck at it at first. I've seen you skate, remember? But it's seawater, not pavement. You fall off, you get wet, you get back up, and you paddle out to the line-up. You wanna do this?"

How could I not take him up on it? A world-class surfer was willing to show me the ropes. I nodded yes.

"Good. 'Cause I got an agenda. And I want you to be part of it."

That sounded mysterious and nothing like the old Dave who had dropped out of competitions and business success and lived in a raggedy van by the beach. No, Dave had dropped back into the world of surfing and commerce and, from the looks of his home, he was doing very well. I learned later what his true agenda was for me.

So, yeah, that summer I learned to surf. At first I did suck, but then so does everyone. But I kept at it. I learned about catching waves, standing up, bottom turns, trimming, and ultimately nose riding. I grew to understand the nature of waves and wind, swell direction, beach breaks and point breaks, and even how to avoid or handle asshole surfers who hogged waves or tried to give me a hard time. My parents loved the idea, and that summer I only worked part-time in the evenings at a convenience store, selling junk food and overpriced canned goods. And the odd can of Red Bull or Fire. Every time some kid bought a can of Fire, I looked him in the eye and asked him a question that only Zeke could answer. It was just a game. I don't know what I was expecting. Once I even asked a kid with a skateboard if he liked older women. The kid shot me a look that could fry bacon. "Freak," he said. "How do they let assholes like you get jobs like this?"

And then there was the final year of high school. I surfed some through the chilly winter but it wasn't the same. Dave was on the competition circuit: Fiji, Australia, South Africa, Hawaii. He sent me emails with famous quotes about surfing.

Like this one by a guy named Gary Sirota: *There are no more committed people on the planet than surfers. We fall down a lot. We turn around, paddle back out, and do it over and over again. Unlike anything else in life, the stoke of surfing is so high that the failures quickly fade from memory.*

Or this one by Bill Hamilton: *I like to tell people who never surf that surfing is like taking a shower, except it lasts a lifetime. We are the lucky few who get to play in God's soup and we are better humans because of it.*

During that final year of school, Sylvia got a letter saying she was accepted to Princeton University. She went on to graduate near the top of our high school class and then move to New Jersey soon after to enrol in summer classes.

That whole school year was a bit of a blur. I kept it steady, though. I did my work. But I never applied to go to university. I didn't know what I wanted to do, but my heart wasn't into the idea of sitting in more classrooms. I knew I wasn't going to just continue my career at the Neighborhood Zipstore, but I was waiting for some kind of inspiration—only I didn't have a clue as to what it was.

I guess you could say I was "letting Sylvia go." We had remained great friends but we both grew to understand we were not in love. We both knew it. There was a sadness between us now, both of us realizing she would go off to school far away and I would wander off into some unknown wilderness once the doors of high school closed for me forever. And there was no Promised Land in sight.

Even Harlem was accepted at a big university. He was really excited. He showed me a list of all the courses he planned to take and, even before high school was over, he had begun to pack his things for fall. "I'm not gonna let anyone there call me Harlem Poodle. Never again." Like Sylvia, he was embarking on a new life and, like her, he was excited at the prospect.

Graduation day came and went.

I crossed the stage.

I shook hands with the principal, who had given a surprisingly cool speech about "embracing ambiguity, curiosity, courage, and compassion."

My parents were thrilled.

Sylvia found me standing alone in the mass of kids in gowns after the event. She kissed me and said, "I'll never forget you. I'll never forget us." And that sounded so surreal, so final, that I thought I might fall into the abyss after all.

Instead, my parents came over and gave me the kind of hugs that only parents can give.

And Dave arrived in a restored 1957 Chevy wagon with a couple of nose riders on top. He honked the horn and yelled my way: "Dixon! Let's surf!"

I looked at Sylvia and she smiled. My folks just nodded, and so I slipped out of the gown and jogged to the car, my cap still on my head, the tassel bouncing before my eyes.

CHAPTER

SIXTEEN

The waves were pure and clear and overhead. Dave and I surfed our brains out that day and it was just what the doctor ordered. We drove to the point break outside of town. Past the Strand and just before you got to the Island of Dogs—Victoria Point. Six-foot-high tubing hollow walls of sea, my feet planted firmly on the nose of Salvation. I'd found gracefulness as a surfer and shared the waves gladly, and when I had a long steep wall all to myself, I found myself saying, "Thank you" out loud, to no one in particular and everything in general.

After our surf session, after Dave had shaken his long shaggy hair like a dog who had just run out of a lake, he said enigmatically, "Now it's time to give back." At least, that's what I remember him saying, although those may not have been the exact words.

Dave had taken charge of his surfboard and surf clothing business again, and he had a knack for it in promotion and design that worked ridiculously well. On the side, he created a foundation he called "Surfers for Peace," but it wasn't so much about surfers protesting war. Instead, it was about teaching kids living in poverty how to surf. He'd sign up any kid from the worst parts of town. Black kids. Hispanic kids. Kids with drug problems. Gang refugees. Bullies. Victims. Kids with mental illness. He knew how to find them and he knew how to get them into the water. And he believed it would change them.

And in many cases it did.

And, as the program really took off, I got to be a full-time surf instructor. And that changed my life.

It's amazing what a little saltwater, a wetsuit, and the ability to handle a surfboard can do to someone. It's nothing short of transformation. And no one was transformed more than me. I'd found my calling.

When winter arrived, Dave moved his operation from place to place in the Southern Hemisphere and I went with him. No more surf competitions for him after that. He had people running his business and he could devote more time to surf camps in parts of the world where they were needed most.

A lot happened in the years beyond that. I worked with a lot of kids between the ages of ten and seventeen in quite a few countries. Dave came up with the most unlikely places. We spent a month in the Gaza Strip, teaching Jewish and

Arab kids to surf together. The more outrageous the idea, the better Dave liked it. The better I liked it. I became, like him, a nomad, happy to hang my hat wherever the job took me. It was the best damn job in the world. Soon, I realized I no longer had any need for pharmaceuticals to keep my head straight.

On my third trip to South Africa, we lined up a number of well-respected local surfers to join us, to teach a few dozen black kids from one of the poorest communities, a place called Thembalethu. We drove the kids to the beach at a town named Wilderness. Even though they had grown up only a few miles from there, many of them had never seen the ocean.

I was working with a group of ten-year-old boys and girls. There was one little guy whose name was Corey who had this great spirit about him. He spoke mostly Afrikaans but a little English, too. And he watched me like a hawk, mimicking some of my body language and repeating words I said out loud. There was something about this kid. I knew his parents were dead and he was living with an aunt in a corrugated metal shanty in the part of Thembalethu called Silvertown. His twin sister, Kathleen, was here as well. She seemed to be fluent in both English and Afrikaans and asked me where I was from and what it was like there. I tried to explain what life was like at home. She looked at me as if I must be lying. Like the other kids, though, they were both most appreciative of all we were doing for them.

Like I say, these were little kids and we were at the beach and it was a fairly calm day. They weren't anywhere near ready to surf. They needed to learn to swim first. We'd spent some time playing in the tidal pools and, between lessons, the kids waded in the shallow waters of the ocean, laughing and splashing each other.

I was sitting on the beach, answering questions from another little boy, when I heard a scream. Kathleen was pointing out to sea and yelling, "Corey, Corey, Corey!"

I knew immediately what had happened. A rip current had formed in these unpredictable waters of the Indian Ocean, and Corey had gone too far into the deeper water and was swept out to sea. It happened so quickly. One minute, everything is fine. The next minute, a rip can form and pull you far from shore.

I saw him, a lone little boy's bobbing head, already far out in the ocean.

I grabbed my board and bolted for the shoreline. By the time I was in the water, I saw Corey go under and not come up. I paddled harder than I'd ever paddled in my life.

When I arrived at the last place I had seen him, I dove down. Visibility was bad and I soon discovered my leash held me back. I had to dive deeper. I surfaced, ripped the leash off my leg, and dove deeper yet. Nothing.

I felt panic setting in. Then a familiar old feeling. One I hadn't felt since high school. Hopelessness. Despair.

I fought it. I focused. Dove a third time. Then a fourth.

It was murky down deep and the currents tugged me one way and another. I felt the futility of it all, searching for a drowning kid in a vast ocean with powerful currents pulling one way and another. I was ready to surface for more oxygen and hope that others would arrive to help. But that's when I had a gut feeling to stay down, go deeper. Just a little deeper.

Fighting the panic in my brain, I did just that.

And then I bumped into something, I reached out and grabbed for it. It was Corey. I had grabbed onto his arm. My lungs bursting, I shot to the surface.

I held him up out of the water as much as I could, as if some magic would happen and the sun would make him start breathing. But he didn't. He felt lifeless in my arms.

My board had drifted away, further out to sea. I saw three of the South African surfers paddling my way, though. I swam clumsily toward them, realizing every second mattered.

On shore, I began CPR on poor little Corey as his sister hovered. It didn't seem to do any good at first, but then his body started to shake and he began to cough. I was in the middle of giving the poor kid his next breath when he vomited all over my face. It was the happiest moment of my life.

Some kids were crying and I heard the siren of an ambulance heading our way. Corey didn't cry. Instead he finally opened his eyes and gave me the strangest look. And then he smiled.

He started to wipe the puke off my face and said, "I sorry, Mr. Dixon."

I just gave him a hug and he hugged back. "You my friend," he said. "Good friend."

Little Kathleen pushed her way through the crowd of other kids, leaned down, and whispered something in his ear. "What did you see?" she said. And then I think she repeated the question in Afrikaans. It seemed like an odd thing at the time. All I cared about was that Corey was alive.

The ambulance had arrived and the paramedics were running on the sand, although I was pretty sure their services were not needed. I leaned closer toward Corey to hear his answer, but all I heard was a word I didn't understand. It sounded like Alice. I wondered if maybe that was Corey's mother. Or maybe it was Allah. Maybe Corey was Muslim—I just didn't know.

Despite Corey's objections, a paramedic whose nametag said *Elton* insisted he be taken for examination. I wasn't going to argue with that. Corey was clinging to me so I was more than happy to go along for the ride. Kathleen came with us as well. She wasn't going to let her brother out of her sight.

Sitting in the back of the ambulance, Corey lay on the gurney exhausted. He closed his eyes and I looked at Elton.

Elton looked my way and said, "He's okay, man. He resting. We're good."

I took a deep breath and Elton laughed in that way that only black South Africans can laugh when some crazy thing has just happened but everybody is okay.

"Alice," I said out loud just then, trying to repeat the word Corey had said.

"What you say, my friend?"

"Ullus or Alice or Allas. It's what he told his sister. What does it mean?"

Elton looked puzzled. Then he looked at Corey, whose

eyes were wide open now as he stared at the roof of the ambulance with a big smile on his face.

"Oh, you mean *alles*," Elton said, a big smile planted on his face, "It's Afrikaans, man. It means all or everything."

And just then Corey began to laugh.

ACKNOWLEDGMENTS

Poetry quotations come from *The Waste Land* by T.S. Eliot, published as a 64-page book by Horace Liveright, New York, 1922.

Photo credit: Daniel Abriel

INTERVIEW WITH

LESLEY CHOYCE

To what extent is Dixon Carter an unreliable narrator in the early sections of this story, particularly in his assessment of his friends and family?

Dixon is "reliable" to the extent that he is giving us a ruthlessly honest and scathing account of the world as he sees it—school, society, life, and those around him. If we buy into his version of things, we get to live vicariously inside his head and see things through his eyes. In some ways, I didn't want him to be too likeable and that is always a gamble when creating a protagonist. But he needed to be interesting and complex enough that we would want to see what his weird journey is like.

As we become his close "friend" and ally, we probably do begin to see that Dixon's view of things may not be the way that things really are. And that should make the story more interesting if I have succeeded. But I had to be careful that I wasn't writing a story where the cursed author tries to trick the reader in any way.

Ultimately, then, the reader has to buy into the fact that the *author* is reliable and that the story is leading to some important revelations that transcend the mere telling of the tale. I'm not sure I succeeded at that. But I tried. And, as with my other novels, once the protagonist finds his voice, I knew he was going to take over anyway and tell the story his way, not mine.

Though we know that Dixon is on medication for a condition he has, that condition is never defined. Why did you decide not to put a clinical name to his medical issues?

Once a person is labeled with an illness or condition, that label seems to color and define who they are and everything they do. I wanted the reader to get to know Dixon as a unique but troubled young man and not be influenced by how a psychologist would describe him. Our understanding of the human mind and mental disorders keeps changing and, while naming disorders is convenient, it is not always accurate. People who were at one time considered crazy might today be considered geniuses and vice versa. Dixon doesn't want to be labeled and judged and nor do most of us. I wanted him to be a unique, very bright but distressed individual trying to cope with the world the best he can.

The first section of the story shows Dixon Carter dealing with one kind of problem, the second with a completely different order of challenge. In what way is Zeke's death a necessary part of Dixon finding out who he really is?

Zeke seemed like a fairly minor character at first. But then I realized he had a very positive influence on the much darker Dixon. He had an intriguing personal philosophy, a cool attitude, and an aura about him. In many ways, he moved through the world gracefully and lived by his own rules. Dixon had much to learn from Zeke and instinctively latched onto him as a friend. He didn't discover Zeke was a kind of mentor and guru until after his friend was dead.

Sometimes we don't realize how influential people are on our lives until they are gone.

Zeke's death is a shock, but his legacy lives on. By way of technology, he gets to communicate from the dead. Unlike most of us, he has actually been able to envision a world after he was gone and wanted to continue to be part of the lives of those he was close to. He knew that he needed to provide some kind of guidance for Dixon and thus recorded his speech to be viewed after his passing.

Zeke knows that Dixon has to get his ass out of the wasteland he is in or he won't survive. Of course, Zeke didn't want to die, but he wanted to be sure that Dixon would change whether he was around or not. It would also seem that Zeke was more connected with some form of the spiritual world and Dixon was not. We all need some spiritual connection, I think, to sustain us. That was part of

Zeke's gift to Dixon and what sent Dixon on a more positive quest.

As Dixon wrestles with the death of his best friend, he's "visited" by his deceased school bus driver friend. Why did you decide this was the best way of illustrating Dixon's early stages of mourning his loss?

I think that dreams reveal so much to us about our deepest fears and aspirations and much more. So often, they seem trivial and, more often, they don't seem to make much sense. Recently I had a vivid dream where I was sitting down at a picnic table eating cold ham sandwiches with Adolf Hitler and Jesse Owens in Berlin in 1936. When I woke up, I realized that I had been reading about Owens and the 1936 Olympics and that was the source of some of it. But why was I there with them and why were we having a picnic eating ham? I haven't deciphered this one and maybe it's just a jumble of thoughts, but my subconscious sure wanted me to see that scene. And, no, I don't think I was "visited" by Hitler or Owens.

On the other hand, there is this. Once, a long time ago, I was surfing big Pacific waves way out of my league in Haleiwa on the north shore of Oahu. I got slammed by a big wave and was pulled under and held there by the churning white water above for a really long time. I struggled to surface but kept getting pushed down. When I was out of oxygen and and was just about to black out, I heard the calm voice of my dead grandmother, Minnie, who said something like,

"Yes, you are in a bad place and if you don't make it, it's going to be okay. There's nothing to fear. But if you want to live, you need to relax and let yourself sink." This of course seemed illogical and counter-intuitive to my frantic brain. But I did as she suggested: relaxed, sank, and then was released from the grip of the wave so I could surface. I had truly been visited by my grandmother. My mother gave me a clear indication, too, that she was still around the day after she died last year.

Harlem Poodle is a bizarrely humorous character. Again, why did you decide that introducing this character was the best way of bringing about Zeke's "resurrection"?

Harlem was a character from another novel I had started and then given up on. I was looking for a very odd and challenging young guy who lived very much in his own world. Other kids had twisted his name around into something more absurd than it already was and he had decided to make the best of it. Kids do that sometimes.

He had his own set of psychological challenges and seemed well matched to team up with Dixon from the Dark Side to bring a whole new perspective on the death of Zeke. So, despite the fact that Harlem didn't get his own novel, he too had a resurrection in this book and served the story well. He is also a survivor, despite the fact that he wasn't "normal" to others and he didn't fit in well. Ultimately, he was the disciple of Zeke to guide Dixon to his enlightenment.

The motif for the story is provided by lines from the famous poem by T.S. Eliot, "The Waste Land." In what way was this poem important to you as a young man?

Well, I had read Eliot in high school and university and never really warmed up to the poetry or the poet. But I found "The Love Song of J. Alfred Prufrock" challenging and unique and "The Waste Land" was baffling, complex, and disturbing. It spoke of hopelessness and despair and, when you are young, you have many troubling moments when it all seems so pointless and hopeless.

I would return to "The Waste Land" as a poet to mine the possibilities of what Eliot was doing and, while I still can't say I love the poem, I find it to be a wonderfully cryptic guide leading to some very interesting mysteries, background stories, history, and ideas.

I had no idea how the poem would fit into the book but I let each fragmented quote act as a springboard for what might happen next in the narrative. So, in some ways, those quotes shaped the story's arc. I don't know, maybe I could have chosen random quotes from newspapers or books. In writing novels, I think you can use almost anything as a cue to suggest what should happen next. For this book, I wanted a literary thread so I used Eliot but, in the end, the story should stand on its own, whether the reader knows the poem or not.

I guess I was trying to create some strange and fascinating puzzle for me, the author, to solve, even though I had no idea what the end product would be or what the rules of the puzzle/game were.

In the end, Dixon finds his fulfilment in learning to surf— and then using his skill to teach and encourage others. You are a surfer and I wonder whether you have similarly encouraged young people to find their own answers on the board.

I was surprised to discover that Dixon learned to surf. He needed something physical and challenging, and Fairweather Dave, another disciple of Zeke, was the mentor to get Dixon in the water and then provide him with some inspiration to get out of his dark little room and go out into the big bright watery world and do some good.

I was even more surprised to see Dixon in South Africa and I guess I know the reason he ended up there. Here in North America, we have so much of everything and many of us are still so unhappy. I met many people in South Africa (and elsewhere) who had very little in the way of comfort or possessions and yet seemed amazingly happy to be alive. To the author, it seemed like a proper job to send Dixon, the surf instructor, to South Africa to connect with some impoverished kids and offer what he could: free surf lessons. In return, they teach Dixon as well.

Surfing teaches many worthwhile lessons to the kids but the gift back to Dixon for getting so involved with helping others is immense. Indeed, a big part of Dixon's "salvation" is his ability to stop wallowing in self-pity and self-loathing and help others.

I sometimes complain about the crowds of surfers here at my home beach of Lawrencetown, Nova Scotia. It's not like the old days. But part of me is thrilled that so many young people are taking up surfing rather than sitting at home playing video games or locked into the prisons of social media.

As I noted earlier, there is a spiritual subtext running through the story. I didn't intend that, but as the book was ending, I realized it was there. Dixon and I were both rather shocked. There are infinite paths to enlightenment and surfing may well be one of them. But it's damn hard work, too. If you have an ocean and can swim, check it out. If you don't have an ocean, maybe it's skateboarding. Or possibly something else.

I heard of a South African paramedic named "Elton" from you some time ago. Are you planning to bring him into a future literary project?

Elton is based on a real person I met in South Africa, a young man who grew up in an orphanage and went on to be trained as a paramedic. He followed his dream and ended up helping injured and sick people, delivering babies and saving lives. I've written a kid's book based on his life and hope to polish it up in the near future for publication.

Thank you, Lesley.